PENGUIN BOOKS

There Once Lived a Mother Who Loved Her Children, Until They Moved Back In

LUDMILLA PETRUSHEVSKAYA was born in 1938 in Moscow, where she still lives. She is the author of more than fifteen volumes of prose, including the *New York Times* bestseller *There Once Lived a Woman Who Tried to Kill Her Neighbor's Baby: Scary Fairy Tales*, which won a World Fantasy Award and was one of *New York* magazine's Ten Best Books of the Year and one of NPR's Five Best Works of Foreign Fiction, and *There Once Lived a Girl Who Seduced Her Sister's Husband, and He Hanged Himself: Love Stories*. A singular force in modern Russian fiction, she is also a playwright whose work has been staged by leading theater companies all over the world. In 2002 she received Russia's most prestigious prize, the Triumph, for lifetime achievement.

ANNA SUMMERS is the coeditor and cotranslator of Ludmilla Petrushevskaya's *There Once Lived a Woman Who Tried to Kill Her Neighbor's Baby: Scary Fairy Tales* and the editor and translator of Petrushevskaya's *There Once Lived a Girl Who Seduced Her Sister's Husband, and He Hanged Himself: Love Stories*. Born and raised in Moscow, she now lives in Cambridge, Massachusetts, where she is the literary editor of *The Baffler*.

There Once Lived a *Mother* Who *Loved* Her Children, Until They *Moved* Back In

THREE NOVELLAS ABOUT FAMILY

LUDMILLA PETRUSHEVSKAYA

Translated with an Introduction by
ANNA SUMMERS

PENGUIN BOOKS

PENGUIN BOOKS
Published by the Penguin Group
Penguin Group (USA) LLC
375 Hudson Street
New York, New York 10014

USA | Canada | UK | Ireland | Australia | New Zealand | India | South Africa | China
penguin.com
A Penguin Random House Company

First published in Penguin Books 2014

In the original Russian "Among Friends" and "The Time Is Night" were published
in issues of *Novy Mir* and "Chocolates with Liqueur" in the collection *The Goddess
Parka* (Vagrius, Moscow). Anna Summers' translation of "Among Friends"
appeared in *The Baffler.*

Published with the support of the Institute for Literary Translation (Russia)

LIBRARY OF CONGRESS CATALOGING-IN-PUBLICATION DATA
Petrushevskaia, Liudmila
[Novellas. Selections. English. 2014]
There once lived a mother who loved her children, until they moved
back in : three novellas about family / Ludmilla Petrushevskaya ; translated
by Anna Summers ; introduction by Anna Summers.
pages cm
ISBN 978-0-14-312166-4 (paperback)
1. Petrushevskaia, Liudmila—Translations into English.   2. Domestic fiction, Russian—
Translations into English.   I. Summers, Anna, translator.   II. Petrushevskaia, Liudmila.
Vremia noch'. English.   III. Petrushevskaia, Liudmila. Konfety s likerom. English.
IV. Petrushevskaia, Liudmila. Svoi krug. English.   V. Title.   VI. Title: Time is night.
VII. Title: Chocolates with liqueur.   VIII. Title: Among friends.
PG3485.E724A2 2014
891.73'44—dc23   2014012797

Printed in the United States of America
1 3 5 7 9 10 8 6 4 2

Set in Stempel Garamond
Designed by Spring Hoteling

This translation is dedicated to
my loving husband, John,
and to the memories of my mother,
Irina Viktorovna Malakhova,
and grandmother
Klavdiya Kirillovna Malakhova.

Contents

Introduction

Russian is a story-swapping culture. Bring your children to a playground, sit yourself down on a bench next to other sunflower-seed-crunching moms, and in ten minutes you'll know whose husband drinks, whose younger sister got pregnant by an unknown party, and who was insulted, again, by her mother-in-law, because they all live together, and so on. But some stories a stranger won't hear. Shameful stories—shameful by Russian standards; stories that mix violence, insanity, and jail. What they call *extremal* in Russian—stories too extreme for casual tale-swapping, suitable only for furtive whispering.

For example, a family of five, say, is living in a three-room apartment in Moscow in the mideighties. They have just enough. Mother and father work, the roof doesn't leak, there are staples in the cupboards, an occasional delicacy in the fridge. There are even two crystal vases on the shelves. One day, while the grandmother and the children are out at a New Year's pageant, the mother tries to kill the father with an ax. That's it. The father disappears to the ER; the mother disappears to a hospital for the insane, to await trial; the crystal vases get sold to pay for the mother's defense; six months later the mother comes home to a wasteland. With her remaining strength she tries to raise the children, while the grandmother grows more and more demented; finally the mother gets cancer. The end.

This would make a typical Ludmilla Petrushevskaya story. But it also happened in my house, to my family, many years ago. We didn't know at the time there were stories written for us, about us; in the Soviet Union, as the narrator in *Among Friends* notes wryly, everyone lived as though on a desert island, and especially families like mine, families traumatized—and stigmatized—by *extremal*. Petrushevskaya's work was suppressed for decades; only later, after the Soviet Union's collapse, did we find out that all those years when we knew only shame and neglect, in the same city a woman exactly my mother's age, also a mother, was composing story after story and play after play about families like ours—ordinary families who had suffered a tragedy.

The three novellas in this volume tell extreme stories that couldn't be heard for many years—censorship wouldn't allow it. Petrushevskaya was unable to publish *Among Friends* for seventeen years; it existed as samizdat. *The Time Is Night* was published in Germany in translation before it came out in Russia. When *Among Friends* and *The Time Is Night* finally appeared, they weren't alone: a whole wave of previously suppressed works was released at the same time. It turned out that a number of brilliant writers had been trying to tell their own extreme tales about life in the Soviet Union, which was so opaque, so completely shrouded from both the West and its own citizens, that it was impossible to tell what was happening next door, let alone in Siberia. Fedor Abramov wrote about the devastation in the Russian countryside, the sufferings of the millions of peasants; Chinghiz Aitmatov about the government corruption and environmental disasters in Central Asia; Sergei Dovlatov about the horrors of army life; Aleksandr Solzhenitsyn and Varlam Shalamov about arrests, interrogations, political prisons, and camps; Andrey Platonov about the civil war and the Bolshevik revolution.

And Petrushevskaya? She described in minute detail how ordinary people, Muscovites, lived from day to day in their identical cramped apartments: how they loved, how they dreamed, how they raised their children, how they took care of their elders, and how they died. She spoke for all those who suffered domestic hell in silence, the way Solzhenitsyn spoke for the countless nameless political prisoners. To write about, say, the woman next door who worked for the post office, some bedraggled Aunt Masha who was left by her husband to raise three children on a salary of ninety rubles when a pair of shoes cost twenty, if you could find them, and who had to care for her paralyzed mother while her teenage son wreaked havoc (all details from Petrushevskaya's stories), took as much art and as much courage as describing one day in the life of Ivan Denisovich. The difference was that Petrushevskaya's subjects were closer to home—they weren't exiled out of our sight, out of our mind. They lived across the hall; they shared the room with us; they were my mother and grandmother.

As both her critics and admirers agree, reading Petrushevskaya is an unforgettable experience. This testifies to the exceptional power of her art, because her characters, by their own admission, don't make particularly fascinating subjects. In this volume, her heroines are tired, scared, impoverished women who have been devastated by domestic tragedies and who see little beyond the question, How to raise a child? How to feed it, clothe it, educate it when there is no strength left and no resources? Such women are boring even to themselves. Anna, the heroine of *The Time Is Night*, complains that no one wants to know how she lives: not her former friends or colleagues, not the state, not her neighbors—she herself can barely stand it. No one wants to know, except for Petrushevskaya. She takes it upon herself to describe her drab characters in such a way that we can't put the book down, and when we finish reading we are overwhelmed by the most profound empathy.

Nowhere does Petrushevskaya accomplish this feat of imagination more completely than in *The Time Is Night* (1992), with her portrait of Anna (who, like Solzhenitsyn's Ivan Denisovich, doesn't have a last name, only a patronymic), an unemployed and unpublished poet on the cusp of old age, living in a cramped two-room apartment with her little grandson. Her mother is in a hospital for the insane; her two grown-up children constantly threaten to move in with her—one of them does so, at the very end, depriving Anna of the last vestiges of privacy.

A brief prologue indicates she's talking to us from beyond the grave, but leaves us to wonder how and when she died. Some commentators have assumed from the overwhelming pressure conveyed in Anna's monologue that her death was a suicide. Petrushevskaya denies this interpretation. In a sense, though, the manner of death hardly matters. Whether she died the next day or stumbled around for several more years fulfilling her duties, the part of herself that mattered most to her fades away after the last sentence, where she bids good-bye to "all the living" who have left her. *The Time Is Night* is, indeed, the story of two Annas. One is a tall woman with an exhausted face, poorly dressed, with neglected teeth, whose hands smell of cooking oil, and who can't walk past you without making an uninvited comment. She torments her poor daughter but allows her worthless son to manipulate her and rob her. She commits tactless blunders and downright cruelties. This is Anna the hag. But there is another Anna, the one who is telling us all these unattractive facts about herself with such objectivity and humor, and whose sad but rich inner life envelops us the moment we start reading her posthumous diary. This is Anna the poet. It is this Anna that dies at the end of the diary, leaving the hag behind to stumble around a bit longer.

Duality is also contained in the heroine's name, and her occupation. Petrushevskaya named her after the great Russian poet Anna Akhmatova, who had suffered similar tragedies, yet endured for a very long time. The other poet mentioned is Marina Tsvetaeva, who did in fact kill herself. Petrushevskaya saw her Anna vacillating between Akhmatova's stoic endurance and Tsvetaeva's ultimate self-destruction. Anna's life is objectively extremely hard—life during Stagnation (1964–82) was hard for everyone who wasn't the ruling elite, and the divorced, unemployed Anna belongs to the most vulnerable and marginalized part of the population. Her tragedies are marked by *extremal*: her son has been to jail for a violent crime; her mother is dying from schizophrenia; her daughter is homeless. Still, the reader can't fail to notice that some of her problems are self-induced and that despite everything there are many joys available to her. There is her adored grandson; there is her daughter who could be her friend; there are her books, her walks; and, finally, there is her poetry. The famous line by Akhmatova, "If only people knew from what muck poetry grows," comes to mind throughout the novella. Anna has a gift, as did Akhmatova, as did Tsvetaeva, as do all talented poets, to translate the filth and muck of reality into harmonious verse. This gift, we are convinced, might have saved her had it been nourished.

The other monologue in this collection, *Among Friends* (1988), is Petrushevskaya's best-known and most controversial work. The story it tells is so extreme—by peculiar Russian standards—that it wouldn't be shared even in a whisper. Many critics and readers interpret it as an attack on Russia's two revered institutions: friendship and motherhood. To this day Petrushevskaya gets criticized at public appearances for her heroine's behavior.

The novella's heroine, who narrates the story,

believes herself to be dying. She lives with an estranged husband, who finally files for divorce, and a young son. Her parents are dead; all she has by way of family is a group of old friends who have known one another since college. It is their custom to convene every Friday in a little apartment that belongs to a married couple, the nucleus of their club. Throughout Russia's imperial and Soviet history, such unofficial networks were a beloved recourse among intelligentsia, allowing them to speak their minds freely—something they couldn't do anywhere else in a censored society. Petrushevskaya's "friends," however, are deeply apolitical and don't seem to take notice of anything outside their club, including the Soviet invasion of Czechoslovakia. Behind their cynicism and snobbishness they think themselves invulnerable, yet when a patrolman pays them a visit they are too terrified to even use the bathroom. In the end, all illusions and pretenses come undone, and cozy gatherings turn into a snake pit. In the notorious closing scene that still sends readers into a fury, the desperate narrator performs an act of violence toward her son, because she believes it to be the only way to ensure that her so-called friends don't abandon him after her death.

The more recent *Chocolates with Liqueur* (2002) was conceived as a homage to Petrushevskaya's favorite author, Edgar Allan Poe. This is the first time it appears in English. Its subject is violence against a woman and her children that's committed daily, inside an ordinary home, in view of the numerous neighbors. One of Petrushevskaya's scariest stories, *Chocolates* is narrated in a light, conversational manner, which makes the novella all the more frightening.

The heroine is Lelia, a young mother of two who is trying to protect herself and her children from a murderous, psychotic husband. Unfortunately the husband owns the apartment they live in, so Lelia has nowhere to go. The abuse carries on for years, unobserved by anyone. Only the neighbor's pet, a German shepherd, senses Lelia's fear, and in the end it is the dog that saves Lelia and her children. Why Lelia agreed to marry her husband in the first place is part of the novella's mystery. She could have been pregnant by another (we are given to understand), or else she, an orphan without family or friends, could have been flattered by the young man's persistent attention. The chief instrument of his seduction is chocolate filled with sweet liqueur—impoverished Lelia's favorite treat. The chocolate is an allusion to the Poe story "The Cask of Amontillado," on which this novella is based. In it the perpetrator similarly lures his victim into a mortal trap using the victim's love of sweet wine; in both stories the crime is committed inside a respectable residential building. Out of fear for her children's lives, Lelia is unable even to call for help during the final attack and is prepared to suffer death in silence, another mute victim of domestic tragedy.

What makes reading Petrushevskaya so disturbing yet so compelling, so depressing yet so exalting? Partly it is her exceptional eye for (often painful) detail. Partly it is the mordantly witty asides of her narrators, both sympathetic and unsympathetic. Perhaps most of all it is what we might call the courage of genius, the willingness to attempt to turn even the extremities of suffering and degradation into lucid, compassionate art. Family and friendship are inescapable and natural, and yet they are also, under these circumstances, hellish and ugly. Those who endure this extreme misery are usually mute. Petrushevskaya endured it, too, but by a kind of miracle was somehow endowed with a power of perception or sympathy, which didn't exempt her from the misery but at least allowed her to record it. All that immense quantity of suffering and squalor would be lost, would disappear into a historical void, if it hadn't found a laureate in her. Suffering is bad enough, but permanent invisibility is even worse. It mitigates the horror, in some mysterious way, when it is witnessed, recorded, transfigured.

ANNA SUMMERS

There Once
Lived a *Mother*
Who *Loved* Her Children,
Until They *Moved* Back In

The Time Is Night

A woman called me, a stranger. "My mother"—she paused—"has left some papers. She was a poet. Can I send them to you? No? I understand." Two weeks later I received a folder full of scrap paper, pages torn from school notebooks, even telegram blanks. There was no address or last name. The handwriting on the folder read, Notes from the Edge of the Table. *Here they are.*

My little boy doesn't know how to behave at other people's homes: he touches everything, asks for seconds at the table; he finds a dusty toy car under a bed and wants to keep it. "Look, Grandma, I found myself a present!" The rightful owner, a tall boy of nine, wants it back, and an argument ensues. I drag my Tima to the bathroom; he is crying inconsolably. We came to borrow a few rubles; next time they won't let us in. Even tonight my dear Masha took her time at the peephole, and all due to Tima. I carry myself like the Queen of England and refuse Masha's offer of tea with crackers, but my belly rumbles loudly and I sneak pieces of baguette from my shopping bag. I need to feed Tima: I stuff him with the offered crackers and ask for extra butter—they forgot to hide their butter dish. Oksana, Masha's daughter, interrogates me about my eternal pain—my Alena—right in front of Tima.

"Does Alena ever visit you, Aunt Anna? Tima, do you ever see your mommy?"

"No, dear, Alena is home with mastitis."

"Mastitis?" Oksana raises her eyebrows. Whose baby exactly has caused Alena's mastitis?

I grab Tima, plus a few crackers, and we flee to the living room, to the television. Oksana follows on our heels. She tells me I must complain to Alena's boss that she deserted Tima. So leaving him with me means desertion? I remind Oksana that Alena is not working, that she is at home with a new baby. Finally Oksana asks me about the baby's father. Is it the same man Alena told her about when she called to borrow for a down payment but they were buying a new car and renovating their dacha? The one who makes her weep with happiness? Him? I tell her I don't know.

The implication is clear: we shouldn't come around anymore. They used to be friends, Oksana and my Alena. We took a vacation together to the Baltic—me, young and tanned, with my husband and both children, and Masha with her Oksana. Masha was recovering from an especially tumultuous affair with a certain professor of Marxism-Leninism, who, even after Masha had aborted his child, wouldn't give up his wife and other girlfriends, including a fashion model in Leningrad. I stirred the pot further by telling Masha about another woman of his, famous for her wide hips, whom I once saw running after his car as he tossed her an envelope with some cash—dollars, it turned out, but not very many. In the end Masha stayed with her Oksana, and my husband and I entertained her that summer, and she let us pay for her drinks despite her large sapphire earrings. Even all those years ago, I'm trying to say, even before I was fired, Masha and I occupied different rungs on the social ladder. This will never change.

Right now her son-in-law is trying to watch soccer; her grandson, Denis, is bawling, demanding his nightly cartoon—the scene repeats itself every evening, apparently; that's why everyone's so tense. Tima, who watches this program at best once a year, appeals to the son-in-law, "Please, I beg you!" and drops to his knees—he is copying me. Alas.

The son-in-law dislikes Tima and is clearly tired of Denis. Between you and me, Oksana's husband is on his way out, which explains Oksana's venom. He is writing a dissertation on Marxism-Leninism—the subject seems to cling to this family. Masha, true, publishes pretty much anything. She threw me a few crumbs in the past, some odd jobs, although it was I who covered her back when she urgently needed a piece on the bicentennial of the Minsk Tractor Plant. My fee was surprisingly small—I must have had a coauthor, some chief engineer from the plant. That piece, however, was the end of me. The next five years I was told not to show up at that publisher, for someone had made a comment along the lines of, What bicentennial? Have we all lost our minds? Do we really think the first Russian tractor came off the conveyor belt in the eighteenth century?

Tonight's an important soccer game. Denis is on the floor, weeping. Tima rushes to help, pressing buttons with his clumsy fingers, and the screen goes black. The son-in-law runs to the kitchen to complain; Denis quickly restores the screen's picture, and the two are sitting on the floor watching peacefully, while Tima laughs with strained eagerness.

The son-in-law must have threatened divorce, for Masha enters the room with the expression of someone who has done a kindness and now regrets it. The son-in-law is peering over her shoulder. He has a handsome face, a mix of gorilla and Charles Darwin; at the moment gorilla dominates. The women are yelling at Denis; by yelling at Denis they are, of course, yelling at us. Two women yelling—that's nothing new for my poor boy. He just stands there, his mouth twitching—a nervous tic.

My poor little orphan. It was even worse at the house of a distant acquaintance, a former colleague of Alena's. They were having dinner when we barged in; Tima squawked that he was hungry. I hurried to apologize—the child is hungry from all the walking, we'll leave in a moment, just wanted to see if there was any news from Alena. But they offered us borscht, thick, meaty borscht, and then the second course. More gratitude on my part—nothing for us, thanks; well, maybe just a little for Tima; Timochka, do you want some meat? At this point a giant German shepherd jumped up from under the table and bit Tima on the elbow. Tima bawled, his mouth stuffed with precious meat. The father of the house, who also looked like Darwin, yelled at the dog, but in fact he was yelling at us, for barging in. An ugly, ugly scene. That's it, there's no going back for us. I've been saving this house for the rainiest day.

Alena, Alena. My faraway daughter, where are you? There is nothing more precious than love. How I loved Alena! How I loved Andrey! Infinitely, absolutely. What have I done except love them both?

It's too late now, my life is over, although the other day someone called me "young lady" from behind. I turned around: a fatso in a tracksuit, unshaven and sweaty. "Sorry, ma'am, I'm looking for this address. Can you help? We need to spend the night somewhere; the hotels are full." Right. I know the type. For a pound of pomegranates he'll want a bed with clean sheets, hot water for tea, a million other things. I can see five moves ahead like a chess player. But I'm a poet. Some prefer *poetess*, but both my idols, Marina and Anna, called themselves poets, so on the rare occasion when I give a reading I ask to be introduced as poet Anna—and my married name. And how they listen, those children! I know a child's heart. Tima is always with me; he refuses to sit in the audience, wants to be onstage next to me.... Very soon they'll stop inviting me altogether; again, because of him.

My happiness, my little one. So quiet at times. A difficult, unhappy childhood you've had so far. You smell of flowers. When you were little I used to say that your potty smelled like a wild meadow, your unwashed hair of phlox. After a bath a child's scent is impossible to describe. Silky hair, silky skin. I know nothing lovelier than a child. Where I used to work, this one idiot used to say that baby cheeks would make a great handbag. She absolutely adored her son and used to say that his bottom was so perfect she couldn't stop looking at it. That perfect bottom is now serving in the army, his days of adoration long over.

How fast everything wilts! How helpless I feel

looking in the mirror. I haven't changed, I'm still the same, but here is Tima telling me, Grandma, let's go—wanting us to leave the moment we arrive at my reading, jealous of my so-called success. But I must work, my little one—your Anna needs to provide for you, and for Granny Sima; Alena, at least, is using your child support and doesn't bleed me for more. But Andrey, my beloved son, what about him? I must give him something, mustn't I? For his injured foot (more on this later), for his life ruined in prison. Eleven rubles a reading. Sometimes seven. But still, even twice a month, it's something. Thank God for Nadya, this angel of kindness who throws readings my way. Once I sent Andrey to take my invoices to her, and imagine, the scoundrel borrowed ten rubles from the poor woman, who has a paralyzed mother on her hands! How I wagged my tail, how I begged her forgiveness! I know, I whispered to her in a room full of people, my mother, too, in a hospital all these years.

How many years? Seven. Seven years. Once a week I go there to feed her; she gulps down everything, cries, complains that her roommates steal her food. But how can they? None of them walk, the head nurse told me; and you, she added firmly, you are muddying the waters here, agitating the patients. After I hadn't come for a month—Tima was sick—again she told me: Don't come anymore. Don't.

Andrey won't leave me alone. He comes every month and demands his share—of what? Why, I ask him, do you keep robbing me and the little one and Granny? Then, he tells me, I'll rent my room out for x amount. What room? I demand for the hundredth time. What room? Who is registered here? Myself, my mother, Alena with her two children, and only then you, and you live at your wife's. You can claim fifty square feet here, that's all. In that case, he replies, I want the price of those square feet. In that case, I reply calmly, I'll sue you for alimony, as your mother. In that case, he retorts, I'll report that you already receive alimony— from Tima's dad. He doesn't know I receive nothing— Alena takes it all! If he knew, he'd do something stupid like go to her office and file a complaint. Alena understands this and stays away, stays quiet, and rents a room somewhere for herself and the baby. What does she live on? I can tell you exactly. Tima's child support is x; as a nursing mother she receives y from the state; as a single mother, z. How she lives on this sum I cannot fathom. Does her baby's father pay rent? She doesn't tell me whom she lives with or even whether she lives with anyone; she just cries. Since the birth of baby number two we have seen her twice. On her most recent visit we re-enacted the famous scene from *Anna Karenina*— Anna's reunion with her son. I played the evil husband. The visit took place because I'd asked the "girls" at the post office to tell Alena, when she showed up, that she had to leave Tima's money alone. On the day the money arrived, Alena showed up on our doorstep, purple with rage, pushing a red stroller (*So we have a baby girl* flashed through my mind). That's it, she yelled, pack him up; we are getting the fuck out of here! Tima started whimpering like a puppy. I'll never forget, as long as I live: the child swaying on his thin legs, wailing in misery, torn between the two of us. I spoke calmly to her. I told her she had abandoned her son, leaving him with me, an old woman; that for fifty rubles I could see her checking her son into a mental institution. You, she interrupted, you gave your mother away; *your* mother is in an institution. And why did I do it? I asked her. Because of you and yours—a nod toward Tima. Then her new fatherless brat started wailing. Breaking into sobs, my daughter enumerated the sums she lived on, as if to say that we, Tima and I, were living here in luxury, while she was homeless. A home for her, I told her calmly, should come from the dick that knocked her up and then skipped off because no one can stand her two days in a row. She grabbed the tablecloth and threw it at me, but there was nothing on the table, and a tablecloth cannot kill anyone.

That was right before my pension, which arrives two days after Tima's child support. I can't have Tima's money, Alena announced, because it won't be

LUDMILLA PETRUSHEVSKAYA

spent on Tima. On who then? I wailed back. Go to the kitchen and see for yourself what's in our pantry: half a loaf and fish chowder. So I wailed, wondering in a panic whether she had somehow found out about my gift of pills to a certain Stranger, who had approached me two weeks earlier outside the Central drugstore. Tall, with graying temples, face swollen and dark. Help me, he whispered, my horse is dying. What horse? His favorite horse, it turned out. He was a jockey, and his horse was ill. The drugstore was sending him to the vet pharmacy, which was closed. And the horse was dying. He needed at least some Pyramidon, but they wouldn't sell him enough pills. At this he swayed, grabbing my shoulder to steady himself, and I felt the weight of his hand, a man's hand. I flew up the steps to the second floor, where I lied through my teeth to the young pharmacist about three sick grandchildren, for whom I needed triple the allowed amount. I paid with my own money—a trifling amount, but still the Stranger couldn't come up with it. Instead he carefully wrote down my address on a matchbox with the pen I gave him, and then kissed my hand, which smelled, oh, shame, of the cooking oil I use in lieu of unaffordable creams. As I was placing three sheets of pills in his swollen hand, another man appeared out of the blue and pulled the

12

Stranger away. Before they reached the corner they'd swallowed all the pills from one sheet. Strange, indeed. Who consumes Pyramidon in such doses? Or had I been duped? Was it possible that the horse didn't exist? The mystery will be solved when the Stranger appears at my door.

On whom, I wailed at my daughter, on whom do I spend money? "Him, of course," she replied, choking back bitter tears. "Always him: your darling Andrey." What was there to say? "Eat with us." We finished the last scraps of food, and hurray, my daughter forked over a few rubles. Then she took her most recent fatherless creation and nursed her in my room, among the books and manuscripts. I peeked in: a fat, ugly child—a replica, it appeared, of her deputy director, who happened to be the father. I learned this heartbreaking fact from her diary, which I discovered by chance among my old notebooks. Alena looked into every nook and corner of my room—I worried that she might take my books to sell. But she was looking for this, for ten pages of the worst news.

I beg you: don't ever read this, even after I die.

Last night I fell so low, I wept all morning. For the first time I woke up in a strange bed, put on yesterday's clothes. He even asked what I was being so shy about.

What, indeed. Everything that was part of me last night—his smell, his skin—became alien and disgusting after he told me that, begging my pardon, he had an appointment at ten, he had a train to meet (with his wife on it, I guessed). I lied that I also had an appointment, at eleven, and went into the bathroom to cry. I wept in the shower, washing him off my body. Inside, everything swelled, burned, and ached.

(Nine months later we knew why.)

This is the end, I thought. He doesn't need or want me, but I cannot live without him. All that's left to do is throw myself under some train.

(Because of *this*?)

I called Mom last night as soon as I got here. I told her I'd be staying at Lenka's, and she replied, "Which Lenka this time?" and said I was welcome to stay at this Lenka's, since I liked him so much.

(What I actually told her was, "How can you? We need you here—you are a mother, after all! Your baby's sick, etc." But she interrupted me with "okay, bye" and hung up.)

. . .

I put down the receiver with a polite grimace, but he didn't notice my embarrassment. He was pouring wine, looking as though he were trying to come to a decision. I shouldn't have told him so directly that I was staying, that I wanted to give all of myself to him, a stupid cow.

(Exactly!)

He stood there, frozen, while I didn't care anymore. It wasn't like I'd suddenly lost control, no. From the beginning I knew I'd follow this man. I knew he was our deputy director of research—I'd seen him at staff meetings. At lunch at the cafeteria, I was shocked when he, an important figure in our institute and much older than I was, chose to sit next to me. He was joined by his best buddy. (Girls from this weirdo's lab told me that in the middle of intercourse he suddenly yells, "Don't look!" then hides in the corner; what it means they don't know.) The buddy immediately began to work on me, while the deputy director just sat there and then suddenly stepped on my foot.

(I can feel my hair going gray. And this is my daughter writing! That night, I remember, I woke up because

Tima had a terrible, hacking cough. He was turning blue before my eyes, unable to breathe; then, terrified, he began to cry. I had gone through this with my children: acute pharyngitis. The first thing to do was to sit him down, submerge his feet in warm water, and call an ambulance. But one person cannot do everything at once. The line is always busy, it takes a second person to get through, and look what the second person is up to in the meantime!)

Then he pressed my foot again, smiling into his coffee. I felt hot and almost choked. It's been only two years since my divorce, but nobody knows that Shura hadn't touched me after that one time. We slept in the same bed, but that was it.

(What nonsense. What matters is that I saved the boy that night. I calmed him down, told him to take little breaths through his nose, then ran very hot water in the shower, and we sat in the steamy bathroom, all sweaty, but it helped. My love! I'll always be by your side. A woman is timid and indecisive when she alone is concerned, but she turns into a tigress when something threatens her children. And what is your mother telling us here?)

He wouldn't touch me. I didn't know anything then.

. . .

(Bastard! Bastard!)

I was relieved. I was so exhausted with the baby, my back hurt, I was bleeding for two months. There was no one to ask—among my girlfriends I was the first to give birth. I thought it was normal.

(You should have asked your mother. I would have told you that the bastard was terrified of another pregnancy.)

He slept next to me, ate, drank tea (burped, peed, picked his nose), shaved (his favorite occupation), read, wrote his term papers, slept some more, snoring gently, while I adored him and was ready to kiss his feet. What did I know? What?

(Take pity on the poor darling!)

I knew only that one time, on the farm, when he proposed to go for a walk after dinner. It was white nights, the sun never set, we walked and talked, and ended up in the hayloft. Why did he choose me? That day we worked on the same row of potatoes; suddenly my Lenka yelled out, Careful! I turned around and saw right behind me a huge dog with something ugly and enormous pointing at me.

. . .

(That's what you get for sending your daughters to a farm!)

I leaped aside, and Shura shooed it away with a shovel. What are you doing tonight? he asked. "Don't know." In the evening we climbed up to the hayloft. He pulled me up. Then he hugged me. We sat like that for a while, like idiots. I kept telling him to stop, that I didn't want that. Then we heard a noise, and he lowered my head and covered me with his body like a child. I felt so warm next to him. It was as if we'd found each other after a long separation. This is love, I kept thinking. We no longer cared who was making that noise (mice, it turned out). He whispered that it hurt only the first time, that I needed to be strong, and he kept pushing into the bloody mess, the straw underneath me all wet—he must have tried every trick he'd heard about in college. I was squeaking like a rubber toy, but was thinking only of him, afraid he'd get tired and leave. I loved him like my son.

(If only!)

Later he said there was nothing more beautiful than a woman. And I couldn't stop stroking him, he had become part of me; this time we didn't hurry, he wanted to reach the end. I knew I was leading him in the right direction, and finally he reached his destination, and I stopped squeaking—that's it....

(That's it, indeed. Children, children....)

Pleasure, that's what it's like. Please, don't ever read this. He twitched and trembled, moaned, then pressed himself to me and whispered, "I love you."

(Love? *Love?*)

Later, at first light, he nodded off, and I pulled myself up and shuffled to the pond to rinse my bloody camisole. Then Shura walked over, too, naked and bloody. We washed each other off and for a long time bathed in the warm brown water. And that's how our best student, Veronica, found us—she was always the first to come to the pond to brush her teeth. She saw my bloodied cami, looked at us with crazy eyes, and ran. Shura dove from shock. I hurried to wash my clothes; Shura pulled his on and left. It was that moment that scared him for life. That's it. He never touched me again.

(And out of this filth and blood came innocent Tima, who is gorgeous like a Greek god, despite what they say—that beautiful children come out of only loving unions. No, I want her children to read this—but later, when they grow up. Let them know *what* I was and *what* she was! I'll put it back on the wardrobe; she'll find it eventually. Never have I let a man hurt me. And what do we read here? She calls *this* suffering? This nonsense? I'll allow myself a digression. From this, from what my poor daughter describes here, moans and pain and blood, comes to life a little cell, and this cell is each of us. Oh, great mother nature! Why do you have to trick us? Why do you need all this mucus, stench, violence, our sleepless nights and exhausting work? Presumably to make things right, but nothing ever turns out right.)

I was standing in the shower, weeping, in the apartment of our deputy director, a serious man in glasses. Suddenly he climbed into the tub; I barely had time to toss my wet panties over the shower curtain. He looked at me in silence, panting heavily, while I was weeping, pleading that he must go, that he'll be late. I could no longer imagine myself without him and just wanted this moment to last forever. . . .

(*Mamma mia.* What is this, could somebody please tell me? Next to her I'm a little lamb. And this is her second man. Men must sense her willingness to flop on her back as soon as they so much as glance at her.)

He dressed me and dried my hair. I started crying again, almost delirious, like years ago, when Papa was leaving us for good and I hugged his knees and Mom was pulling me away, telling him to get lost, telling me to have some pride before this scum.

(Her own father she compares to this . . . this father of her bastard!)

He flew around the apartment, picking up every crumb, every little hair, all while telling me to write to his PO box. Then he changed the sheets and rolled around on the clean ones, to give the impression of deep, solitary sleep. He packed the used, stained sheets and gave them to me. "Here, have them washed," he said. "And then?" He paused. "As the situation dictates," he pronounced finally.

(Why not just let her keep the damn sheets? So this is what she washed, boiled, and ironed! And then—get this!—she actually returned them. And she was right: such men can't bear the smallest expense.)

When we were ready to leave, he glanced with longing at his marital bed, then at me, and it was clear that all he wanted was an excuse to undress me again. But then he simply pulled down my tights. After that he told me to walk up one flight and only then to call the elevator. When I walked outside he was already gone. Only on the subway did I remember that I'd left my wet panties on the shower curtain!

(Probably knew what she was doing, ha-ha. The wife comes back, hop, a homecoming gift drops on her head—to slap her dear hubby with! And him—he had to use her again, already dressed, since she was there for the taking, gratis. Where's your pride, Alena? Why don't you say no?)

Imagining his wife with my wet panties, I felt my hair stand on end. It's nighttime, and I'm choking with shame. How I betrayed him! I'll never forget how he looked at me in the cafeteria, how he pressed down on my foot and then put his hand on my knee, but I pushed it off. How he and his buddy walked me to the door and suddenly he said he needed to discuss a few things with me and then scribbled a time and the address. I went there the same night. How happy I felt! On my way there I felt so happy! And what a sad, shameful ending!

But that wasn't the ending; it was the beginning. The ending came later. Soon after the described events, Tima and I lost sight of our young mother, who was taking final exams, finishing her internship under this same deputy director at the research institute, where she was also defending her thesis, ostensibly, but really spending all her time with this much older man. When she finally came home she announced she wanted to talk.

"Good. Me too."

"I'm getting married."

"How so? Is he a polygamist? One can't be married to everyone at once."

"You don't understand."

"What don't I understand? Has he divorced his wife?"

"That's not the point, Mama!"

"It's not? So do you intend to be the mistress of a married man?"

"We are going to have a baby. He's renting an apartment for us."

"Who's us? What about him? Where's he going to live?"

"I can't bring him here, can I? And I'm not taking you with me," she said with familiar hatred. "Tima, yes, but not you!"

She didn't take me, but she took Tima's child support. Not right away—later, when it became clear that her so-called husband wasn't going to spend a dime on her. Such men's love is always platonic, immaterial. They always need their money for themselves. They'll starve to save a penny! They are always saving for some major purchase—computer, video camera, car— and they love to get married for free, flattering themselves that their sperm represents some kind of investment. So this is whom we were feeding. My poor deceived daughter, where are you?

The time is night. The little one's asleep. I continue to defend the gates against Alena's occasional onslaughts. Last New Year—I'll never forget—she showed up with a present for Tima: the ugliest blue plastic monster on the planet. But Tima covered it with kisses, played with it all night, and I didn't have the heart to tell him that his mother had shamelessly taken two boxes of Christmas ornaments, leaving us with only three. No one had invited us over; we stayed home as always. In the evening we went to the Christmas tree vendor to collect branches off the floor for a bouquet, which we decorated with handmade garlands. Luckily my daughter had missed the box with the Christmas lights and Tima's favorite ornament: a little glass house with a glittering roof and two windows. I turned on the lights, the glass house sparkled, and Tima and I, plus the blue monster, walked a slow circle dance around our bouquet as I wiped away tears.

We exchanged presents. Tima had wrapped a drawing in an old newspaper, and I had made a rag doll for his puppet theater, his fourth. These dolls are very difficult to make. I always have trouble with faces, especially noses, and in the end just paint a comma. But I can't always be knitting, gluing, and drawing something for him. He wants to make things himself, he tries, but he's too clumsy and impatient; after a few minutes everything is a tangled mess. But I'm busy! I need to work! In response his mouth twitches nervously.

I tried to give Andrey a present, too—a pamphlet on decorum with underlined passages. He rejected it rudely and demanded his usual price. And again he threatened to jump. He made this threat not to me but to his wife—she must have insulted him again. He has jumped before, without a warning, from their second-floor window—heavily intoxicated, it turned out. He broke both legs and damaged—permanently, it appears—a nerve in his heel. The pain is unbearable, his wife tells me, although on the surface there is nothing, not even a scratch. He is incapable of any work that requires standing, which rules out pretty much everything except night watchman. It was five years ago that it happened. A tragedy.

I'm afraid of both of them, husband and wife. On the phone she tells me everything's fine—last night Andrey ripped a sleeve off her robe again. She's a nurse—hard, hard work, but she gives Andrey shots for his heel, and massages. And he's still so young! They both are—Alena and Andrey. On her last visit I told Alena, You've got to take care of yourself! Look what you've turned into! She looked away, slowly welling up with tears and hatred, then got up without a word and rolled out the heavy carriage with her new fat bastard. Dragged it down four floors—absence of elevator is our curse.

This jealousy toward Andrey—she had it as a child, but later it passed. As teenagers they grew closer and talked in the kitchen late at night. How much I wanted to be a part of their youth, their dialogue, but the kitchen door was closed to me, as were their hearts. When Andrey went to prison, she sent him letters; I'll talk about them later. Yes, she did write for a while, until she brought home that bum of hers, Shura of the Southern Provinces, who ate every scrap of food, completely oblivious. Every morning for thirty minutes he massaged himself with an electric razor—his idea of meditation. Tima screaming in a wet diaper; Alena trying to use the toilet; Andrey, fresh from prison, barred from both bathroom and toilet, boiling in the kitchen, where he slept. He jumped a year later, but that was at his wife's, not our overcrowded home.

The day he got out, I waited at the gate—wrong gate. He walked out still in his garb; I had his clothes with me. I ran home, and there he was, dressed in all gray, the prison cap in front of him on the table. Spring, warm weather, streets full of people—everyone must have stared. Pale and thin, chapped mouth—gorgeous beyond words. I knelt before him, unlaced his shoes. And who is this? he asked quietly. I wouldn't have come if I'd known, he said, after I told him just what I thought of his brother-in-law and what it had cost me to marry him to Alena. At that moment Provinces scrambled past the kitchen and into the bathroom like a frightened bunny and began banging on the rusted latch, trying to lock it.

Tima was born in June. Sixteen days later Andrey came home. Oh, what a mess it was. I'd just managed to marry Alena and Provinces, barely, with the help of their classmates who worked with them at the farm. In the end, college authorities threatened him with expulsion and immediate draft if he refused to marry. Such were the sad facts. But finally he arrived. He flopped at our kitchen table without even a glance in my direction. Alena was there, eight months pregnant, with greasy hair and bags under her eyes. "Alena," I said, "what's the matter? Haven't you been pregnant before? Go wash your hair! I didn't look like a scarecrow when I carried you!" (It's true: I'd never let myself go like that—clean hair always and a fresh complexion whenever possible.)

"Honey," she informed him, "remember: Mommy's nuts." Her intended drooped a little and took cover in our only bedroom, where he proceeded to polish off all the food in the house—Alena didn't get a crumb. "The kid sure has a healthy appetite. Eat mine, then," I told her quietly. She glared at me, tears welling, and sobbed that she hated me, hated, hated!

"Why, what did I say? Provinces came to the capital undernourished, I understand, but you are carrying a little one. He must pay his way—or is he planning to live off me? I'm a poet; I don't make much, as you know."

"A goddamn graphomaniac is what you are."

I didn't know then—how could I?—that she was carrying *him*, my Tima, Timothy, named after someone in Provinces' family. I'd wait on her hand and foot, if she'd let me, but the thought of Andrey was tearing me to pieces, and I simply couldn't provide for them all: her and her baby, plus that husband of hers, that coward who married her only to avoid the draft and expulsion. (He feared army rape, but think of what my poor son must have gone through in jail! Who's going to pay for his suffering?)

So they got married. I set out a spread in the bedroom: salad, pasta, and a pie with dried fruit. Their two witnesses were present—not the ones from the potato field; our husband had turned these down. Next morning my dear daughter was in the kitchen bright and early, scrambling our last three eggs for her beloved, standing over him with a napkin like a footman. I told her later, "Look, waitress, I had three eggs for the two of us, for pancakes. Now there's nothing left to eat. Let him pay something, anything, or did he marry you for room and board? Make some oatmeal for yourself, at least. How are you going to feed the baby? Look at your breasts!" I wanted to hug her and have a cry together, but she pushed me away.

And that's how it went, our life together. Alena used all her strength to please her beloved, as she called him. Her beloved! I stopped leaving my room, and I turned off the fridge: first, to save energy, and second, what was I expected to do, her abandoned and insulted mother, when after a day waiting in food lines and then lugging home two heavy bags of groceries I return from a library the next day into a complete wasteland? A wasteland left behind by their endless guests, who visited the impoverished young couple in hordes, she proudly feeding them *their* sausage, cooked with *their* butter, filling our little apartment with gutwrenching aromas. They even snatched my teakettle! I subsisted on boiled water with plain bread, the same food my son lived on in his cell, and my daughter explained away my passing to and from the kitchen with pots of boiled water with "Mom's off her rocker."

But my hatred for Provinces, it turned out, was

the glue that kept their family together. To be honest, all I wanted was for them to disappear, to vanish somewhere and leave the room to Andrey. But where would they go? I told them that I wouldn't allow Provinces to be registered at our address; this way maybe they'd get a room in a dorm for married couples—or had he married her for a Moscow registration? That caused a storm of tears, followed by a counterthreat: she'd stop Andrey from registering here, too. Later she came into my room, tears still falling. I was pretending to work. "Do you want me to die? Is that it?" she asked me. "Go on," I said. "Go on living, you and your future fatherless brat. But let me ask: Is it worth it for your so-called family to exist at the expense of homeless Andrey and your granny hospitalized?"

She cried so easily back then. Tears streamed from her bright eyes, my sweet darling's eyes. I tried to hug her, and this time she let me. "Fine," she said. "I know you don't want us here, me and my baby; all you ever wanted was that criminal son of yours; you just wish I'd vanish, cease to exist. But that won't happen, you understand? And if anything happens to my precious, your Andrey will go away for much longer." So that's how she spoke of Andrey, who alone shielded eight friends with his sentence; for whom she used to shed tears every night; her suffering brother, to whom she wrote those lovely, funny letters. (She wouldn't let me see them, but I read them anyway, admiring her talent; I quoted her once as a joke, and oh, what a scene she threw, accusing me of spying and God knows what else—what a terrible, terrible scene.) True, she did cry over Andrey the first two months; the rest of the time she had every reason to cry over herself. And now we were all expecting an amnesty, in honor of Victory Day.

With the last of my money I bought a lock for my room and invited a friendly plumber to install it. He charged me one ruble and joked that he was looking for a wife. What a dear, simple soul! He didn't realize that I was quite old and almost a grandmother! The next day he showed up, fortified with drink, with a bag of candy in an outstretched hand, and was greeted by Alena's loud phooey. My suitor vanished for good—he even resigned from our building. Well, declared my daughter when the door closed on him, what we just witnessed was a perfect example of a man on the hunt for a Moscow registration. I should be careful not to contract genital lice or some venereal disease, she continued, or she'd bar me from the bathroom and especially from her child—my own Tima!—until, that is, I produced proof of my moral and physical fitness. Because, you see, she had been warned at the maternity clinic about various forms of syphilis that were found, apparently, even in public soda fountains. Thus spoke a (finally) wedded wife who attended classes at the clinic and generally followed the path of virtue.

I left the scene of the battle and locked my door. For a long time I shed bitter tears. I was only fifty years old! My joints were only beginning to ache, my blood pressure was almost normal, I still had my health, my life! And yet—my life began to melt, to ebb away, but let's have mercy, let's leave that part in darkness. . . . You poor old folks, I cry for you. But how I failed to appreciate my relative youth, considering myself an ancient hag! At night, it's true, I couldn't sleep even then, but I didn't give up, not yet. I'd comb the stores for scraps of fabric, hoping to stitch together a skirt or a dress, and I even nursed plans to crochet a blouse from some cheap yarn. Can you imagine? Me, thinking of crocheting, living as I was on a volcano, only moments away from welcoming to our disaster area two beloved beings, Tima and Andrey? I now save those scraps for Tima, for a shirt or something else, but a shirt's too difficult for me, and Masha occasionally gives me her boy's hand-me-downs. Not the nice stuff, but still. And I already have a school uniform stashed away—that's right. I save and save.

Masha, for all her faults, is all I have left from my old life. It's no use talking about it now, about how my friends and colleagues vanished, retreating into their cozy lives after I was unjustly sacked. These days I limit myself to a dignified telephone call once a month and a very occasional raid on their dinner tables, but of that I already spoke. Of my scrimping I spoke, too. Mr. and Mrs. Provinces drew stipends in addition to financial aid, plus their hordes of visitors supplied groceries in exchange for an evening in a warm house, even attempting to stay overnight in their room, on the floor, like some collective family. My two idiots were moved to tears by this behavior, seeing in it proof of their friends' personal devotion to them. But I held my ground firmly and called the police, protesting the presence of hordes after eleven at night; once a whole police squad marched in, demanding to see everyone's IDs. A regular Greek tragedy, with me the chorus. This is what my son was coming home to.

But I didn't wish them ill. I tapped my reserves of oatmeal, the only form of nourishment Provinces disliked, and every morning I made a pot of plain cereal, as though for myself, for my sick liver, and every afternoon I found an empty pot in the sink. How I loved my daughter, all of her, down to her unwashed feet in old slippers, her bony shoulders beneath a threadbare robe—all seen from the back, for she no longer showed me her face. I'd scoop her up in my arms, lay her down on clean sheets under a satin comforter (stashed away for now), so she could spend those last days before birth resting, but she kept trotting to her finals, trying to finish early, appealing to professors with her neat pregnant belly to make concessions for her. News about her reached me in snippets of overheard phone conversations—our phone has a short cord, and I'm not deaf, not yet. So Alena worked on her exams and stuffed her beloved, and I sent letter after cheerful letter to the human sewer where my son was spending his days. I'd grown used to Provinces and begun calling him (to myself) "our dud," in preparation for "our dad." To Andrey I explained away Alena's silence by saying she was overworked, and I mentioned my fears for her health, that she might end up in a hospital, which is exactly what happened.

That night I dragged myself home after a full day at the library working on my courtroom news column—one needs to eat, somehow, and there was no way I could work at home, surrounded on all sides as I was by constant slamming and knocking, plus loud telephone conversations about the new favorite subject: nutty Mom and her syphilitic boyfriend the plumber. This time I came back to a blissful silence—at ten the house was empty. I had dinner, alone, in the kitchen, bathed quietly, and fell into my clean, cool bed, only to wake up, as always, at midnight, this time from a ringing silence. I got up and started pacing in front of their door. In a panic I pushed it open and discovered an untouched bed with a rusty stain on the blue bedspread. My first thought was that he'd killed her; my second, that she'd gone into labor. The dud showed up drunk at two in the morning, staggering past me into the bathroom and vomiting. "What happened? Where's Alena?" I kept asking through the door. He emerged as white as chalk and announced that Alena had given birth.

"Congratulations. A boy or a girl?"

"A boy."

"Where are they?"

"Twenty-Fifth Maternity Ward," and he collapsed like a drunken swine.

I left him where he was. Then I scrubbed the bathroom and for the rest of the night washed and ironed a pile of secondhand baby clothes, the numerous donations solicited by me. The dud meekly took containers of food to Alena every day and even ironed, but every night he disappeared, only to repeat his rendezvous with the toilet. I loosened the purse strings, for the dud had nothing: his father, apparently, had drowned at sea and the mother spent her last days in hospitals. I asked him what was wrong with her; I was scared he'd say she had TB—but no, schizophrenia. Thanks a lot. Alena called from the hospital, her voice weak: the boy was beautiful, she told me; he had curls. (Later I saw those curls—three hairs, the rest of his head smooth and bare, like Chairman Mao's, his eyes like Mao's, too.) I told her that in our family all the men and women were beautiful, she and Andrey especially, and then broke into tears. I cry easily—it's my weakness.

Together the dud and I went to collect our Precious. The nurse brought him out and placed him in the dud's arms; I gave her three rubles and managed, in a stroke of luck, to flag down a cab that had just arrived with a mother-to-be. The poor woman could barely move—her water had broken on the way, and the seat was wet and sticky. I should have walked her to the door, but I was so overjoyed at finding a cab that I almost knocked her over, and was rewarded with a filthy seat. I complained to the driver, and he wiped off the mess, cursing his wretched passenger, who was crawling, semiconscious, the baby's head probably craning between her legs.

I think of her often. The baby, assuming it survived, is six now, and she must be at least forty. Mothers— a sacred word, yet—when it comes down to it, you'll have nothing to say to your brats or they to you. Love them—they'll torture you; don't love them—they'll leave you anyway. End of story.

Sixteen days flew by like a bad dream. Day and night became one. There was constant washing and ironing. My daughter developed cracked nipples, plus constipation, plus mastitis with high fever. Screaming Tima, sick Alena, the shaking dud, and silent me. Imagine: Alena forbade me to touch the baby after I made a simple comment that when I was at the library the dud had again gobbled down all the food. In the morning—surprise, surprise—there was nothing to eat. Why do I have to stuff this throat, too? I appealed to Alena, who was in her warm little room that smelled of milk and fresh diapers, washed by me. My happiness snoozed in the corner. But I was torn to pieces. Andrey was coming home—where would he sleep? What would he eat? How would we manage? I couldn't sleep and woke up in a cold sweat. And the dud was always hanging around, preparing for his finals, ostensibly. For God's sake, my darling girl, kick him out! We'll manage! What do we need him for? To stuff his face with our food? So you could humiliate yourself night after night, begging his forgiveness? But I said only this: "Let him go and make some money. To Siberia, to the Far North, where his daddy had made a living. You are not allowed to sleep with him anyway. I refuse to feed him." I overheard the dud on the phone whispering about long-term construction jobs in the north.

"No," she said. "That's not happening. He is my husband. Go and write your stupid poetry."

"Maybe it's stupid. Maybe. But it's how I feed all of you."

Our conversations always came down to my poetry, of which she was ashamed. But I had to write or my heart would burst.

"Anyway. Let him go. Andrey's coming home. Amnesty's been declared. I saw the lawyer."

"Amnesty doesn't mean anything. Stop talking about it or you'll jinx it!"

"Is that what you're hoping for? That Andrey won't come back? He will. And I don't want him to end up behind bars again, because of the dud!"

I spoke loudly, counting on the minuscule size of our apartment. The dud, it turned out, was standing right behind me, not saying a word, as usual. A lot of sweat was spilled in those first weeks, but at least I saw him, my Precious, I saw him always and in everything. Even in the dud's face I learned to see his mouth, his beautiful, wide brow. The dud had emerged from his provinces with those assets, and he put them to good use. Now he is grazing on greener pastures: he married a foreigner, although his salary, judging by Tima's child support, hasn't increased by much. My Alena was a springboard for him, nothing else, but obvious as it was, it hadn't crossed her mind, and she danced before him on her knees day and night.

But finally the day came, and there was Andrey, sitting at our kitchen table, while the dud was banging on the bathroom door, trying to lock it. I appealed to my son, "Please, my darling, please listen to me. I didn't want to upset you, so I didn't mention in my letters that Alena was pregnant by God knows who."

"Hold on. And who is this dude?"

"Just a minute. I'll tell you from the beginning."

"Can you wait? I'm hungry."

"Here. Here's some soup. Eat. You don't know the worst of it! Here's some bread. Have you washed your hands?"

Silence. We were back at square one: the problem of washing hands. He glared at me and took bread with dirty fingers.

"Fine. As you wish. Anyway, I had to do something."

"About Alena?"

"That's right. It's always up to me!"

"I don't remember you bothering on my behalf."

"Andrey, darling, there's a lot you don't know."

"All I know is that I was the only one to end up in jail, and there were eight of us."

"Don't go there. Please. The story is that you were alone against five, right?"

"I've heard all this before."

"Please. Listen to me. That's why they gave you only two years. If it was eight against one—who, by the way, was thrashed by all of you—"

"He got what he deserved."

"Oh, how wrong you are, how wrong! I saw him at the hospital. Anyway, with eight defendants you would have gotten five years. Minimum."

"Just shut up. Bitch."

"Please, my love, I beg you. You are back. The light of my life is back. My only one. You'll show him, you'll show that bastard!"

More banging in the bathroom—the dud was trying to get out.

"I had to take measures. The girls, her classmates, confirmed what had happened in the hayloft and that she had washed her bloody clothes—"

"Mom, enough! I'm dizzy."

"He married her because of the witnesses. Eat, eat, my love: here's potatoes, herring, butter. He hasn't wolfed down everything yet!" I couldn't cry. "What we've gone through! That bastard. A fatherless wretch from some provincial dump. Barely got accepted into college. If they kick him out he'll be drafted."

"Better the army than prison."

"He doesn't think so."

"So you've snagged yourselves a new sonny. Well done. Bitch."

"Eat, my love, eat. Everything's homemade."

At this moment the fatherless wretch finally

extricated himself from the bathroom and approached Andrey. He offered a hand and said a strange thing: "Glad to see you. Welcome."

Alena burst in, buttoning herself up after a feeding, and threw herself on Andrey's neck.

"What can you do? A silly cow." Andrey smiled.

"Silly cow she is," the dud agreed amicably.

They looked so young, so innocent, so full of hope, even in the squalor of our kitchen. If only they knew what awaited them—and what could possibly await them in this life of ours? Darkness and cold, betrayals and death—and the breathing of my Precious, which alone could provide consolation.

My love. It's a physical pleasure for me to hold his weightless little arm, to gaze into his round blue eyes, with eyelashes so long that even when he sleeps they cast shadows like enormous fans. All parents, and especially grandparents, love little children with a physical, sinful love. The child understands that and becomes callous and spoiled. But what can we do? Nature meant for us to love, and so we love—even the old folks, who just want a little warmth.

So my two darlings were having a reunion in our filthy kitchen, and I wasn't a part of it.

"Andrey," I said, "I object to his registration here. And she, in return, objects to *your* registration."

Oh, the power of words. The reunion was over.

Andrey was shocked. "You do? How can you?"

"Don't worry, it's just a form of protest against her. You know how we live here, like bulls in the ring."

The young parents drooped like wilted flowers and slinked into their room. Andrey resumed eating. I perched opposite him.

"Andrey!"

"Mama!"

"Two minutes, Andrey. It's serious. She wants to register him in our apartment. If she does, he can get a room later, through the courts. That's all he wants, that bastard. She's just a springboard for him, nothing more."

"He's got his looks going for him." (Strange laughter.)

"That he does. He could have anyone—and he will! If it were not for my witnesses . . . But never mind. He'll get something off her—a Moscow registration, at least—and then he'll leave her!"

I was speaking loudly, for I was right. Everything happened exactly as I predicted. But to prove it! To prove it took a lot of effort. For he became attached to Tima, took pride in him, took him for walks, showed him off to their hungry so-called guests. How complicated everything was.

And me? I was left with nothing.

"Keep it in mind," I said to Alena one night,

"your husband has the makings of a pedophile. He loves the boy."

Her jaw dropped.

"He loves the boy, not you," I explained. "It's unnatural."

She laughed with relief, even though a moment ago she was crying—it was eleven, and the dud wasn't home yet. She grabbed the phone and dragged it to her room, leaving the door half open. I was the favorite subject of her conversations, endless like winter evenings.

But how old was I then? I was only fifty. Andrey was twenty, Alena nineteen. I had two of them in two years. I had just been fired from the paper for having an affair with a married poet, the father of three children, whom I had every intention of raising myself, stupid idiot. Naturally the wife went to the editor in chief to complain, and almost immediately they received a long-promised three-room apartment. Until then they had all lived in a single room, including his mother-in-law, and he would work in my room, while my own mother loudly berated him for taking advantage of me. . . . So I resigned and joined a remote archaeological dig, just to get away, and the result was Andrey and Alena. We lived four of us in my room, with my mother behind the wall, while a divorce drama unfolded in my husband's hometown. Then his wife decided to pay us a visit. The doorbell rang; I opened the door, heavily pregnant; and there they were, the wife and his teenage son. Next, the wife smashed the window, slashed her wrists with a shard, my husband tried to grab her, the son squealed, "Don't touch my mama." My mother rushed over with some gauze, then took them to her room to revive them with tea.... It was actually a stroke of luck, the wife's visit. Between us things were deteriorating rapidly: he missed his son, worried about finding work in Moscow, chafed under alimony and child support, and plus there was my swelling belly. But then she shook everything up. Women like her, with an instinct for destruction, they create a lot in the end. I'm one of them, alas.

It all seems like yesterday. I look back on my life—men are like road signs; children mark chronology. Not very attractive, I know, but what is, if you look closely? To Alena, I know, my habits, my verbal expressions are deeply distasteful. Especially the question "Is he good looking?" which I used on the rare occasions when she'd open up about her best friend Lenka's admirers; that was back when she was in eighth grade. All I meant was who in their right mind would approach that Lenka of hers, who at fourteen smelled like army barracks, wore size-ten shoes, and sported a mustache? My Alena (all girls born that year were

Elenas in different variations; this year they are all Katyas) was head over heels for that girl, and strained as our relationship was, I was occasionally treated to a breathless rendition of Lenka's adventures. Until, that is, my inevitable question: Is he good looking?

"Mama! What does that have to do with anything?"

"Well, I just mean that he should, at least, be good looking."

"Huh?"

"Well, it would be a miracle if he was, for who'd want to look twice at an elephant like her?"

"Mama! It's me no one ever looks at."

The classic abandoned-wife complex, common to girls from fatherless families.

"It's true, Mama! Last summer, at the beach, all the Georgians courted her and thought she was eighteen!"

"You're kidding. Eighteen, not thirty?"

"Mama, you make everything sound so vulgar!"

"That's why I'm asking. Lenka's admirer—*he* isn't a Georgian, is he?"

"Just leave me alone," she pleaded, almost crying.

The reason for all this talk was that it was as clear as day that horrible Lenka wasn't worth my daughter's little finger. My little beauty, my warm little nest, who was my consolation when Andrey was wreaking havoc as a teenager. She was nine when her father left; my mother did him in with her nagging. On another dig, he picked up someone else in the same way he picked me up, only this time both children were with him. When they came back Alena confided that everyone loved them so much there, so very much; one woman, Lera, literally cried the last night when they were leaving!

After a month of tense, pimple-producing, long-distance negotiations, my husband left for Krasnodar, and for Lera the crier, in whose studio apartment he is currently living with a stepson plus a blind mother-in-law, so my children don't get invited. As for archaeology, he now travels to digs in Rwanda and Burundi, but Africa is full of AIDS, and there is every reason not to romanticize these trips. As for my mother, she considered our papa a conniving hanger-on and a leech, among other things. How she celebrated when he came for the last time to get his things! How she never passed up the opportunity to remind me that she had told me so! How sweet she was with me, this toothless cobra, who now cries on her pillow and gulps down her food.

I began receiving child support—all of forty rubles. I worked: they let me help out in the poetry department, reading and responding to submissions—a certain Burkin threw me a crumb, a kindly man with permanently shaky hands and cheeks swollen so badly I suspected double inflammation of the gums. A ruble a letter—sometimes I sent off as many as sixty letters a month; plus two of my poems would be published— that was another eighteen rubles.

And this is the consolation my daughter offered when the door closed for the last time behind my husband, and I stood with a burning face and dry eyes, contemplating jumping out the window to greet him outside with my corpse. Mommy, she asked, do I love you? Yes, I told her, you do.

My princess, whose every toe I'd washed and kissed. I adored her curls, her enormous blue eyes—where did her looks go?—which exuded such kindness, such affection, such innocence—all for me, for me alone. All this, all this tenderness was taken from me and thrown at the feet of the horrendous Lenka. Day and night she thought only of Lenka and her demands. Andrey and Alena pummeled each other because Andrey needed to make a call while Alena was waiting for that brat to call—hoping, that is, that she'd call, to tell her if anything was happening, if they were going anywhere, if they had been invited to anyone's birthday party.

My children fought each other tooth and nail— another cute detail of our family life. Only at night could I experience the joy of motherhood. I'd creep over to their beds and listen to their breathing, inhale their scent, adore them in silence.

> *My darlings, my soft ones:*
> *Rest awhile, don't stir.*
> *Your mother is with you,*
> *You are always with her.*

They didn't need my love. Without my care they'd perish within hours, but I was a nuisance. *Paradosk*, as my subliterate neighbor Niura likes to say.

Andrey played soccer and hockey; by ninth grade he had more scars than a feral cat. Other boys would carry him home—unconscious, because local ladies had decided to dig up the lawn and plant carrots, and then fenced off their orchard with invisible wire right at the height of a child's throat. Another time some little angels decided it would be fun to throw a handmade knife, and they threw it right into Andrey's foot. This was after my husband had disappeared in the direction of Krasnodar, and I had a friend over—A.Y., a very attractive man, although a married alcoholic, whose wife regarded me in only one sense—as all wives always. So this A.Y., on seeing Andrey spouting blood all over the stairs (I later washed it off, with my tears), asked him, "What's that, old man, a battle wound?" When, six years later, Andrey didn't come home until two in the morning, and my mother screamed, "Go back where you came from!" and whacked him with a chair, something happened to my heart, I couldn't breathe. In the morning I called A.Y., to ask for advice. "To be on a safe side, call the ambulance, Andrianovna," he told me in the cheerful voice he always used between binges. "But remember, women rarely have heart attacks." This only proved that while recovering from his own heart attack A.Y. never looked into the women's ward. Then he asked Andrey's age. "So you expect him to jump up from a woman's bed screaming, 'Mommy expects me at ten'? I was going to become a father at fifteen, and this one is already sixteen!"

The time is night.

My squawking angel is finally asleep, arms akimbo on the pillow. I'm alone with my scraps of paper and a pencil—pens are beyond my means. Everything is beyond my means now, thanks to Andrey, who has taken me for everything this time. This time wasn't like his previous robberies, when he tried to break down my door and in the end set my mailbox on fire. He was demanding a huge amount, twenty-five rubles, for what he considered his room, and calling me horrible names, the most obscene in the Russian language. I huddled over trembling Tima, covering his ears. Luckily Andrey is a coward, and he left when I yelled that I was calling the police.

My poor son, he can't believe I'm capable of calling the cops on him. He has never recovered after the prison, never come back as a human being. Instead he lives off his so-called friends, those boys he saved with his sentence. Some time ago I received a call from the completely crazy mom of one of the eight friends, Andrey's potential codefendants.

"Is this the apartment of such and such? Hello? Does Andrey such and such live here?"

"Nope. Who's asking?"

"Doesn't matter."

Good-bye, then. But no.

"Where can I find him? Hello? I've tried calling the building where he works."

Persistent hag!

"He now works at a ministry." Let her call human resources at every ministry in town.

"Can I have the number?"

"It's classified."

"This is the mother of his comrade Ivan. When I was out, Andrey stole Ivan's new leather jacket! Hello?"

"I'd advise you to search your son's room. By the way, how come he's not in jail? I've heard Alesha K.'s case is being retried." This Ivan of hers is still wearing the sweater I bought for Andrey's birthday with the last of my money. "By the way," I added, "could Ivan compensate me for the things he stole from me?"

Click.

> *To grovel, to pray*
> *At the feet of a son*
> *Who returned from the dead:*
> *May he stay. May he stay.*

Back from prison that day, Andrey was in our kitchen eating my herring, my potatoes, my bread, himself made with my blood and marrow, yellow and emaciated, terribly tired. I said nothing. "Go take a shower" was hanging on my lips. (Since childhood it has made him feel disgust and humiliation—for what was he worth, dirty and sweaty, compared to me, always clean, who showered twice a day, thank God for the free hot water?)

"I need money."

"What money? I'm feeding three people! And I'm the fourth!"

(Behind a floor molding in my room I had stashed my mother's insurance plus an honorarium for five translations from unknown languages, work that came my way after I dumped my tragic story—son coming out from jail, daughter pregnant, unmarried—on every editor in town.)

"Why don't you take a shower? Want me to run you a bath?"

He stared at my collarbones.

"I bought you some jeans, Soviet made, don't laugh—and a pair of canvas shoes. Go change, but first take a shower."

"I'm fine like this. Just give me money."

"And how much do you need?"

"Fifty. For now."

"Are you off your rocker? Look! All I have is five rubles."

"Then I'll go and kill someone."

"Andrey." My beautiful daughter stood in the doorway. "Come. Shura received his stipend yesterday. This one will choke first." Andrey stomped away with the fifty rubles and didn't come back for two days. When he was gone, our patrolman came asking for him and warned us not to register him. Alena and I panicked and agreed to register both Andrey and her Provinces. Swapped prisoners, so to say.

When Andrey returned he was dressed in a new denim suit and accompanied by two young ladies of such appearance that I gasped for air. Alena took one look at them and quickly retreated into her sweet-smelling nest. The three visitors marched into my room, locked the door, and stayed there for an hour. I knocked and pleaded that I needed my things; all I could think about was my stash behind the molding. When the door finally opened, I met Andrey with my hand outstretched. "Fifty rubles, please."

"What the . . ."

"I reimbursed them."

He was going through the contents of my wardrobe. The sluts were waiting.

"I've packed your things. The suitcase is over there."

Where did you go, my silky baby boy who smelled of phlox and wild chamomile?

"The patrolman stopped by to warn us."

"What the . . ."

"That we must not register you."

"Ah, you . . ."

"Please. Of course we'll register you. Of course."

"Fuck that. I'm getting married. You know what you can do with your registration?"

"Who are you going to marry? These two?"

"Why? You think they'll make bad wives?"

The girls brayed with merriment, revealing missing teeth.

"By the way, where's Granny?"

"I didn't want to put it in a letter. . . . Granny's not well."

"You mean dead?"

"Worse. Much worse. The worst that can happen to a person. Do you understand?"

"But where is she?"

"Kashchenko Asylum. Where else?"

"So you two got rid of her."

He grabbed the suitcase, and they rolled out.

The time is night. Everything's quiet. Only Niura, my neighbor, is pounding soup bones for her children's breakfast.

What's interesting is that Deza Abramovna, the chief at the psychiatric clinic, believes that inside the clinic are mostly normal people who simply lack something. The true lunatics, she told me, are outside. Big deal, I thought at the time, like an idiot. I, too, lack lots of things. Only later did I understand. I would come to her crying that my mother had left the gas on, or almost burned down our apartment, or left meat on the balcony while we were gone for two weeks—we came back and there it was, under the layers of flies and eggs, imagine the smell. That was a frightening time in our lives, when Andrey was summoned daily to the detective's office (I went once and was yelled at), from which he ventured home yellow and lifeless. He was constantly getting calls and being dragged off to meetings—with the parents, I understood later, of his so-called friends, who wanted to convince him to take the blame.

My mother couldn't wrap her poor old mind

around what was happening and only repeated anxiously that the boy didn't look well, that he must eat, or that the girl came home last night with a dirty spot on her coat, she must have laid on her back somewhere. Then her nagging stopped and she disappeared into her room, and Andrey left for yet another interrogation and didn't come back. She didn't even ask where he was. Months passed; she carefully arranged her teeth on a bookshelf, and one day she produced a plastic bag filled with bloodied cotton balls so I could see how many times she spit up blood. What for? Mama! Who, what committee is going to see this? Give it to me—I'll throw it away! Look at yourself: What are you wearing? You have a closet full of clothes; what are you saving them for? For better times, as I understood, for that special day when the door will swing open and she'll come out, young, in a beautiful new dress and everyone will swoon, and then—attention!—someone will marry her (but not some bed-wetting retiree, oh no). Instead, she invited me into her room and whispered that they had come.

"My God. Who?"

"They. The ambulance. Don't yell."

Outside, an ambulance was passing in the rain.

"Yesterday, when I stepped out, they followed. A policeman, too. I turned around and began walking right at him, grinning. I'm not afraid of them!"

My God. I stood frozen in the middle of the kitchen, then shuffled into Alena's room and told her that Granny had lost her mind. She replied that it was I who had lost my mind. Don't worry, I told her, it happens—heredity, nothing you can do. It happened to Granny's sister, who lived a long time, incidentally. Alena rolled out of bed and went to talk to my mother, then came out in tears, shocked. I told her that she, too, needed to be examined, because it runs in the family. I didn't mention to her that I had already invited a psychiatrist, who posed as a regular physician making a house call. During that visit Alena was rude; asked why she was in bed in the middle of the day instead of school, she marched into the bathroom and stayed there until the doctor left.

"You call yourself normal?" I appealed to her. "Look at yourself. Again you missed class. You read all night and can't get up in the morning. This is psychosis. Hereditary. Please, honey." But she just laughed hysterically and slammed the door in my face.

I only said that to shock her into action, to get her out of bed; my heart was bleeding for her. Imagine the horror my life had become: my son in jail, my mother on her way to a crazy house. I simply wanted to drive her out of the trance caused by bad grades, pimples, and some first love of hers, all described in her diary, which I'd read. Here it is.

Please don't read this diary! Mama, Andrey, Granny: if you read this I'll leave—for good.

Yesterday we had a seminar with Tatarskaya. S. sat in front of me and kept looking back, over my head, kind of wistfully, laughing. He and Lenka kidded around; I was just sitting there with a serious expression, trying not to swoon. In the cloakroom Lenka suddenly asked me, "Do you want to get together with S. for New Year's? Because he does." I could barely walk home. S. and I will be together on the thirty-first!

December 22. Again Lenka announced that S. must be in love with me because he often asks about me and refuses to go to the movies if they tell him I'm not going. She looked at me with suspicion, but I let on nothing. Of course I know she loves him; about me she isn't sure. I was so happy I couldn't sleep. Today S. wasn't at school. I must discipline myself! I must stretch in the mornings! Last time S. told me that he got up at noon.

December 30. New Year's Eve is tomorrow. Barely passed exam today. Cried in the hall.

S. finished first and left right away. Gathered up courage and asked Lenka where she and S. were going tomorrow. To the club of the University of Transport, she told me, like it was nothing. S. declared that he hates all-nighters. Lenka bought them two tickets, which included a glass of champagne, a party favor, an American movie, a dance party, and a costume ball. The tickets are sold out, she said. She didn't have enough money for three. I was invited to come along anyway; someone might have an extra ticket. But I'll need a costume: she'll be a gypsy, he a pirate. After this announcement I crawled home like a punished dog. Granny and Mama were fighting. Grandma was screaming that I don't go to bed all night, can't get up on time for my exams. They should be yelling about their precious Andrey, who smokes.

January 1. Sensational news. Lenka and S. weren't at the club. I was there at ten sharp, like an idiot, in Granny's black dress and with a rose in my hair: Granny had dressed me as Carmen. I bought a ticket without any trouble and then shivered in the half-empty hall, watching a so-called concert and a ridiculous dance party until almost midnight. Then bought a glass of champagne, drank it, and left. At home, Mama and Granny were finishing their annual brawl in front of the television. The subject, as usual, was Andrey: he hadn't been home for three days, called earlier, Mama grabbed the phone and really gave it to him—that Granny was going to have a heart attack, they had to call an ambulance, and so on. He hung up, of course, and Granny didn't get a chance to speak to her Only One.

January 5. Lenka showed up at the review before the dialectical materialism exam; told me she'd decided not to go to the costume ball, instead got on the train and spent New Year's in Leningrad with her relatives: little kids squealed, not wanting to go to bed, and Lenka had to discipline them. Tears and misery all over our fair land. S. wasn't at the review.

January 8. I received a C; will have to take it again. There'll be screaming at home—I may lose my stipend. As always, S. answered first, got an A, and left. Lenka reports that

S. called her and told her that he had been at his high school friend's for New Year's; Lenka says he must be gay. We had such a laugh.

January 15. S. came to the library with T.I., who is a junior. Everyone knows she's a slut. They kept smiling at each other, and then S. put his coat over her shoulders. Lenka sat red as a beet, trying to smile. Later we smoked in the bathroom; she cried. I didn't cry, just felt empty inside. Life is a bore, ladies and gentlemen. S., I love you, even though you don't see me. I'd like to give him my photo with just one word: Remember. T.I. is an old slut, twenty years old. I turned seventeen in December. S. will be seventeen in February. He went to first grade at six. Lenka is nineteen. Life's not going to be easy for her, because she's so heavy. She's on a diet now. She has pimples all over her forehead; I do, too, sometimes, but around my nose. She smokes a lot. And she's already slept with boys. She says she knows just as much about sexual positions and such things as the slut T.I. Lenka's convinced S. is gay.

January 18. I'm in bed, pretending to study. Am recording Mama's conversation with Granny in the kitchen. It's teatime.

Mama: You! You've broken all the dishes!

Granny: Me? Me? God help me! What dishes? When?

Mama: Here, look! This cup's missing its handle! There is a plate missing! Where will I buy new ones?

Granny: It wasn't me! Help! Somebody help! Here, I swear on my knees I didn't break anything. (Slowly gets down on her knees.) Here. I swear!

Mama: Oh, stop it, will you. Get up, come on now, get up. It's not a big deal, after all; it's just a plate.

Granny: Help me! (Long moan.) What have I ever broken? (Gets up huffing and puffing, then continues tearfully.) When you broke my blue cup—

Mama: Here we go. Try to remember your difficult childhood, too.

Granny: The only thing I ever broke is the spout on the teapot. (The chair squeaks—she sits down to finish her tea.) That was me, I admit it, but it can be glued! I saved the spout.

Mama: What? What teapot?

Granny: The blue one. We'll glue it on. . . .

Mama: What? The blue teapot? The best teapot in the house? How can we ever use it again?

Granny: You broke my cup, I broke your teapot.

Mama: Alena! Come here.

Me: Mom, I'm studying for the exam. . . .

To confuse Alena further I brought up the subject of pimples. "You see, if you don't wash yourself there and under your armpits, you are bound to get pimples. At the very least you could wash your own underwear. I do the wash after both of you, but Granny has lost her marbles!"

"And I've lost mine," said this pale, slightly pimply young heroine. Everyone is expected to kneel at her feet. But for that she must at least bathe regularly.

"At the very least, you should shower and wash your hair. And use contraception! Use contraception, since you are sleeping with them."

Ah, the power of insults. She was crying now, but for herself, not her crazy grandmother.

That was seven years ago, a lifetime.

The time is night. Today there was a knock on the door. Who is it? Personal business. Great. What business?

Then: "Does such and such live here?" Naming my dear son. Southern accent.

"No, no, and no."

"Where is he?"

"He is renting."

"Give us the address."

Right.

"Then open the door."

"I don't have to open my door without a warrant."

Pause.

"You tell your son, woman, to be very careful."

"Why? Are you a criminal?"

"He's the criminal. We'll find him." Then they kicked the door a few times and scurried away. I counted at least six feet.

I didn't leave the house that day and called

Andrey, who was out of sorts and spoke to me in monosyllables.

"Morning!"

". . ."

"How's your heel?"

"Mm."

"Are you looking for work?"

"Mm."

"Why not?"

". . ."

"Come on, stop it. Smile, will you? Why so down? What happened?"

"Mm."

"You absolutely must get a job."

". . ."

"By the way, someone's looking for you. Again."

"Who? My friends?"

"That's right. Your friends. Said they'd find you sooner or later."

"Who did?"

"Your so-called friends. I told them to go away, that they were criminals."

"And?"

"They answered that it's unclear which of you is a criminal. Andrey! What have you done this time?"

"Me? You nuts? Why me?"

Something had clearly happened.

"Well. They are looking for you. There were six feet in all. Approximately."

"You mean there were three of them?"

"They could be amputees. In any case, you mustn't come around."

"I was about to come for my money."

"Money—from me?"

"Mom, you've made this all up, right?"

"You're funny," and I hung up.

The monthly tribute, which he imagines I owe him, has been paid twice. Now I'm a pauper! The first time he stole my precious childhood book *Little Lord Fauntleroy*. I was saving it for Tima, for when he'll be able to accept the heartbreaking news that the little lord will get nothing. Just once I was able to read to him up to that point, just once. Then the book disappeared. Tima and I waited outside the hospital for Nina to come out after her shift. When she did, she was grumpy. She complained about Andrey, said she couldn't put up with him any longer, that he had to go. It turned out they hadn't paid their utilities for six months. Nina managed to keep the phone working, but their electricity had been shut off. In despair, Andrey came to rob me. Nina agreed to exchange the book for forty rubles. Forty rubles! I always suspected that Nina was one of those two sluts in sunglasses.

That was the last time Andrey visited our nest in

my absence. With the last of my money I installed a new lock, which involved chasing down our district plumber, who finally came with a colleague, took a look at the walls and floor in my hall, and drew the right conclusion about my affairs. The door, he declared, was wrong, the lock didn't fit, the ceiling was too low, but I implored them, telling the truth: that we needed protection from a former convict who was registered here. I didn't cry, just trembled. They quickly lost interest in me; their standard game of claiming the job was impossible without extra pay lost its thrill in the face of my genuine misery. I collapsed behind my new lock, but it didn't prevent Andrey from robbing me once more—he got a taste for milking my miserable ass.

That month we were in a craze: I beat forty more letters out of Burkin, telling him that I owed money, which he understood. Anything else—childbirth, illness, jail—failed to move him. Only booze and money for booze touched his sympathy; my life tragedies only made him uncomfortable. And how lightly I danced around his office! I fluttered from desk to desk, showering everyone with compliments; my face tightened into a youthful smile; my washerwoman hands, calloused like hooves, had been groomed and the nails trimmed. The little one waited downstairs, with the guard—children were not allowed upstairs. There, on the third floor, I was an unrecognized poet, and the alcoholic

Burkin a stern but fair patron of the arts. He ignored my groveling, my "you are my savior" blandishments; he opened and closed his desk drawers, where empty bottles rolled around—a useless hint, since I don't give bribes; I simply can't afford them. He chatted on the phone, stepped out, came back; his beautiful young assistants dropped in one by one and almost flopped on his lap; men from other departments also dropped in to wait for someone to take them to the bar next door, while downstairs Tima was stewing, running out of patience, and I had only one thing on my mind: Letters! Give me letters!

Who knows, maybe those girls were unrecognized poets, too, maybe they too needed letters, but Burkin couldn't support everyone—besides me, the letters fed a widow of one of his friends who had drowned but whose body had never been found, so his two children couldn't get a pension. Burkin taught her how to write five types of answers. The widow wrote: "Dear Comrade: Unfortunately the subject of your poem (novel, short story, novella) doesn't fit our publication." That was answer one. If, miraculously, the subject did fit, "The style leaves room for improvement. Very best."

What kind of letters did I write? I wrote epic poems. My nights were filled with conversations with the invisible authors—all those retirees, sailors, accountants, students, construction workers, inmates, night watchmen. I quoted, advised, praised, criticized extremely sympathetically. When I submitted my letters to Burkin, he looked as if someone had died. But how could I write differently? Behind each manuscript I saw a living person, some of them ill and bedridden, like Nikolai Ostrovski. Sometimes they wrote again, addressing their manuscripts personally to me, but those Burkin firmly set aside for the "Dear Comrade." New authors scared him like fire.

Not long ago I wrote a vignette in prose, surprising myself. It was nighttime, and I was keeping vigil in the kitchen. I wrote in my daughter's voice.

Better like this, in the street. The landlord came to inspect his property, found the toilet seat cracked. He had been working in the Far North making big bucks; now he's back and wants to bring women here, he tells me. You may step out with the baby, or stick around if you want; we'll have a threesome.

(Horrible things come to mind when you imagine your daughter completely helpless! Unfortunately, most of this is true. She herself told me about her landlord and her life in general.)

. . .

I was staying over with Katya at Mama's. In the middle of the night Mama got up, turned on all the lights everywhere, and noisily led the boy to the bathroom: pee, baby, pee, since you've already peed yourself. Then opened the wardrobe in our room, looking for dry underwear. Katya woke up in her stroller; the boy stood shivering, all wet, holding onto her elbow. Skinny bottom, thin legs, a mass of entangled curls—angel. Not a glance in our direction. Katya squeaked. I knew I'd have to get up, so I said, Mama, let me help you find underpants. What can you find here? she screamed back. Bastards, bastards! Told them not to give him water before bed, told them to have some shame and not stuff themselves at our expense, so he has to drink water to fill his belly. Still a beautiful woman, tall, in a torn nightshirt, she yanked her elbow from the boy's fingers, and suddenly he started sobbing, covering his face. Here! she screamed, like a Greek goddess of terror. Here, put these on! Come, sweetie, I'll help you, I mumbled, unable to lift my behind.

Oh no, let him do everything himself, he must learn, I'll be gone soon. Who am I going to leave him with? Then he fell to the floor, sobbing. Katya's squawking intensified, and then off she went with her siren.

. . .

That's the sketch; I portray myself with complete objectivity. The reason behind it was the annual call from my daughter, who, as I've said, lives in some distant outskirt with an illegitimate child by her imaginary lover. So the phone rang, and the boy and I both raced to answer, as usual. I won.

"Mama, it's me."

"Hello, you."

"Right. Mama, my urine test shows protein."

"How many times did I tell you you need to wash regularly? Go take a shower; that will take care of your protein."

Choked laughter. She always laughs like this when she wants to die. Just wait awhile, I'll be laughing, too.

"Mama."

"Talk. I'm listening."

"They want to put me in a hospital."

"What hospital? You have a small child! Go clean yourself up and take the test again."

"Okay, okay. But what if my blood's really bad? What do I do? Lie down and die?"

"Whose blood is good these days? Your own son's hemoglobin is half the norm."

More choked laughter. "Mine's half that."

"What does it matter? We are talking about your

son's health! He's undernourished; he needs liver, he needs walnuts. Stop laughing, you."

"Right. So you think there's nothing to be afraid of?"

"Why are you crying? Stop right now."

"Listen to me." Voice trembling. "I'm due in two weeks. They want to keep me in the hospital until then."

"Nonsense. What did you say?"

"I said I'm high-risk, with high blood pressure plus bad kidneys; what if I croak on the table? What's going to happen to Katya?"

"Huh, big deal! Women in our family aren't easily scared. They tried to scare me, too. I was pregnant with you, and there was little Andrey. So what? Even though I had my mother and your so-called father to take care of him, I refused to be hospitalized and only went when contractions began, at six thirty in the morning. I tried to wake up that father of yours . . ."

"Right. Enough."

". . . he wouldn't get up. Don't go there at all, you hear me? They'll put you on the table to examine you, then poke you for tests and damage the placenta. They want you to give birth earlier; this way they'll pay you less for maternity leave."

"Fine, all right. I'll do as you say. You see, I've arranged for a neighbor to watch Katya for five days. Longer than that she refuses."

"Hang in there, just hang in there. Keep hiding from them; they can't force you."

"Okay then. Bye."

"Okay. Kisses."

Laughter. "How's the boy?"

"What do you care?" And I hung up.

Only then did the horror of what I'd just heard sink in. First, she was pregnant again.

Second, what she really wanted was to leave her fat Katya with me for God knows how long. Dear Lord, what possessed the feverish brain of this hormonal female? What did she need another baby for? How could she not notice, how could she miss the deadline? Easy. Took notice only when the baby started kicking. When a mother breastfeeds she often misses "the arrival of the Red Army," as my daughter and her Lenka used to refer to their periods back in the day. Many get caught that way. The dick pushes ahead, the dick doesn't care about the woman's safety. And who was this dick? That same peripatetic deputy director? Or the local plumber? Or, worst of all, that landlord of hers? And how long could this go on? Naturally no one would give her a late abortion. That must have been when she started making the rounds with her protein and high blood pressure, begging for a late-term abortion, but they dragged her around for tests and then more tests, until it really became too late. As if they were genuinely committed to not squandering a single life. She should have looked for a nurse, for anyone who'd have given her a shot. Lots of women manage it somehow, some as late as the sixth month. Andrey's wife, Nina, told us about her neighbor, who missed her deadline, too, and went to a beach resort instead. Came back, sent her kids away for the weekend, gave birth to a six-month-old fetus, a boy, and left him by an open window. It was October. She went to wash off the blood. He whimpered all night, but she never came to him. By morning he stopped. And the doctor wasn't even there; he'd disappeared right after the shot. But she found someone, a man at that. Why didn't you take care of this? Why do I have to pay now?

Our conversation wasn't about her urine. Our real conversation went like this: Mama, help me, take on one more burden. You have always saved me. Save me this time. But, my dear daughter, I can't betray the little one; I can't force myself to love another creature. Mama, what do I do? Nothing, honey—I've given you everything, my last penny. Oh Mama, how horrible, I'm going to die! No, no, don't say that, you must be strong. Look at me; I stay strong for the little one, for all of you—me, your mother, your only one. The other day someone called me "young lady." Can you imagine? Your mother's still a woman. So you must be strong.

Promise? You can't move in here, you understand that. Again, distorted faces in the mirror in the hall—that's where we always fight, only in addition we'll see him, the innocent lamb, watching his two deities, his mama (me) and his mother (you) hurling obscenities. I live for him, don't you understand? Do you remember when you told me, better in the street than here with me? That was the truth, alas. Okay, Mom, I'm sorry, I'm being an idiot. I love you.

The little one came to me: "Grandma, please stop shaking. Why are you hiding your face?" Like a summer rain, tears gushed out of the two dried wells. My love, my angel, my eternal sun. Meekly he let me cover his face with kisses. Translucent skin; enormous eyelashes and eyes. Gray, almost blue, like Grandma Sima's; mine are like honey. My angel, my gorgeous one.

"Who were you talking to?"

"Does it matter, honey?"

"No, tell me."

"I told you: grown-up stuff."

"Alena? You were screaming at her?"

I feel like a pig. Children are the conscience personified. They ask their little questions, and then they grow up and shut up, and live with the belief that there is nothing one can do, there is nothing anyone can do. I can't do it to the little one.

"Why did you yell that she must wash herself?"

"No, my love. I told her that she must wash the floors!"

"Are you silly?"

"Oh, my love, I am silly, I'm a regular idiot. I love you."

Countless light kisses on the cheeks and forehead, never on the mouth. One should never kiss a child on the mouth. I saw one such parent on a streetcar—he must have been taking his daughter, a girl of five, home from kindergarten. He simply tormented her with kisses! I told him off. He snapped out of it, as did his daughter, who couldn't catch her breath from all the tickling and kissing. He redirected his attention to me and showered me with curses. "Stay out of it, you old bitch; mind your own goddamn business; shut your smelly trap." But I wouldn't stay quiet. "Look what you've done to the child! I can imagine what you do to her at home. Criminal!" The passengers were full of indignation—at me. "What do you care, you old slut! Look at yourself—you are old, old!"

"I only wish her well, this child of yours. People go to jail for this, inappropriate behavior with a minor. Child rape!"

"Stay out of it, old fool!"

"And then you'll be surprised when she gives birth at twelve—and you won't be the father."

I won, I distracted him; now he brims with a new desire: to punch my insolent mug. From now on, every time he wants to lay a hand on his daughter, he'll remember me, and his desire will turn to hatred. Again I've saved a child! I always save someone. In our neighborhood I alone keep vigil at night. One summer night I heard a woman's half-choked "Oh God, someone help!" My hour had come: I stuck my head out the window and announced loudly, "What's going on here? I'm calling the police!" Our local cops, by the way, respond promptly to such calls, when the criminal is still there. Two more windows opened, another voice yelled, and I saw a couple men running in this direction. "Right here, Comrades, you are almost there," I directed them, even though they were at least a hundred yards away. But my goal was to scare the rapist, to make him let go of her. And he jumped out of the shrubs and ran off. The woman burst into tears. Imagine her terror when he started choking her and banging her head against the wall of our building.

And so we win. I bring knowledge to the ignorant masses, I give voice to their conscience, I orate like a Pythia at schools, camps, clubs. And how they tremble! But they listen, and they'll never forget. My eternal misery, my Tima, always sits next to me when I perform, never leaves me alone, and the children receive us as an indivisible entity. Seven rubles with kopecks is my fee—three or four readings a month plus submissions, and one can live, almost. Who can stop a woman trying to feed her child?

This week I'm giving a reading at a children's winter camp outside the city, thanks as always to the wonderful Nadya B., who has arranged it for me. We are being picked up at the propaganda office. They promised us that at the camp we'd be fed, hurray. And then the horror begins. Not the horror itself but the prelude to the horror. The phone rings, and the little one grabs the receiver. "Hullo, hullo.... You want Anna who?" Pause. The phone goes dead. I pounce on the boy: Never, do you hear me, never again ... Phone rings; I grab the receiver and get a painful kick in the shin. The boy flops onto the floor and turns on his siren. My children never allowed themselves such tantrums, but the little one has the nerves of a hysterical woman.

In the meantime a sweet provincial voice informs me that my mother, Serafima Georgievna, will be transferred from the hospital to a facility for the chronically insane.

That's it. That's the end of the line. What I've been too terrified even to imagine has come true.

"How can I address you, dear?"

"Valya."

"Dear Valechka, what happened? Has she been difficult? Where is Deza Abramovna?"

"Deza's on vacation; we are all on vacation starting next month. They are renovating the clinic; all the patients are being moved. Some will go to another hospital, some will go home, the rest will go to a facility for the chronically insane. But your ... your mom, your auntie—"

"Does it matter? She's a human being!"

"Anyway, she cannot go to the hospital—they won't take her. So you've got to decide. The paperwork's ready; tomorrow they are taking her. Don't worry, you don't have to come."

"Is there anyone in the office?" The boy takes a step back and punches me in the kidneys with both fists. "Valechka, dear, what's the urgency?"

My mind is racing. If they move her, we lose her pension. This means we'll be completely and totally screwed. Her pension arrives two days from now—can we still get it? Oh horror, horror. One lives from day to day, admittedly badly, but then something happens and the previous existence seems a quiet harbor. What a disaster. They die like flies at that facility.

Suddenly I hear, "There's no urgency. You were informed a long time ago. Really, you shouldn't worry."

"No one's informed me of anything! Which facility is she going to?"

"Outside the city. We'll get her ready and everything—"

"That's two hours one way!"

"More like three. But there's no need for you to be there. They have everything they need. Okay then, I'll need your signature, but that can be done later."

"What signature?"

"Saying you agree—"

"But I don't agree!"

"Are you taking her home, then?"

"No signature! Forget it!" I hang up.

Now we must hurry to the reading. The usual tantrum unfolds: Tima refuses to put on his warm felt boots with overshoes and a wonderful fur hat that used to be Andrey's. But it's cold outside! Do you want me to stay up all night, bleeding my heart out, while you are in bed sick? I implore you, and so on. In the end we agree on the combination of a flimsy hat and warm boots. Subway tickets cost a fortune, but then we were promised a ride by car. The car turns out to be a drafty pickup truck, but even for this I'm grateful. We are accompanied by a lady in a torn sheepskin coat and a homemade foxtail hat.

"Ma'am, your sleeve's torn. . . ."

"Again! I keep stitching it up. . . ."

Her outfit betrays a feeble effort at luxury, but later she gets paid the same miserly fee as I.

"What are you?" I ask her. "I'm a poet."

"I'm a bard."

"A bard?"

"That's what they call me. I tell stories using puppets. It's very simple: I make these funny puppets with potatoes for a head. Your girl will enjoy it."

Right—can't tell a girl from a boy, this so-called bard, although Tima's curls have confused many. My girl stares with puffy eyes at the window; his hat is off, the car drafty.

"Me, I'm a poet. (Put your hat back on!) A namesake, almost, of the greatest one. . . . (I'll tell the driver to stop the car!)"

"Which greatest poet?" the bard wants to know.

"Guess. I'm Anna Andrianovna. It's like a mark of fate."

"Oh, names are always a mystery! Take mine: Xenia."

"What's the mystery?"

"It means *unknowable to all*."

"Nice one."

My stomach is howling, my heart pounding in alarm. After the call from the hospital I didn't eat; I tried to track down a psychiatrist I knew a long time ago, but at his home they said only "such and such doesn't live here anymore," very bitterly. But I've fed Timochka: sugared bread and cold tea. We call it pastry. He's still hungry, but first we must rattle around in this unheated, stinking tin can, our stomachs rumbling. What a bitter, hungry lot. My mother is still in the hospital, in her bed; she is eating well, I was told on the phone. I've tried to find that Valya, but no Valya seems to be working there. I know how my mother eats: sucks in food greedily with her toothless mouth. Last time I saw her, her shoulders were nothing but bones. Look at her! Let her be, let her die in bed. No. That's when we get punishment—right before the end, when there's so little left of us that it's unclear who's being punished.

"Children are the best audience," the bard drones on. "You arrive: there's chaos, kicking, screaming. But once you begin your story . . ." She is shouting over the roaring engine.

Maybe Nina's playing a practical joke? No, I've checked: tomorrow they are taking her away.

". . . folk tales," Xenia finishes.

"Excuse me, what's your full name?"

"Just call me Xenia."

"Well, it's not really appropriate, is it? When did you retire?"

"Me? I'm not retired yet," answers the fatherless one, who looks like she should have grandchildren.

"I'm retired," I tell her. "When my collection of poems comes out they'll recalculate my pension—I'll be getting more. Tima and I live from hand to mouth, plus my mother is being kicked out of the hospital; my daughter stays home with two little ones, but she has child support for only one, and my son, he's disabled." I recite her a full list of my miseries like a beggar on a train.

"And me," this orphan informs me, "I won a car! I'm learning to drive."

"Right. I've heard about the lawsuits: people buy lottery tickets, then lie about winning; in the end they lose their prizes."

"We have a son," she continues, her cheeks jiggling like jelly. "I'll drive him to music lessons. My husband refuses to drive out of principle, because the lottery ticket was bought by my mother."

"I see, you must have had your son late. But it's okay; by the time you're eighty he'll be all grown up."

"Mama"—sometimes he calls me mama, sometimes grandma—"I'm hungry!"

"Your daughter, would she like a candy?" mumbles this unknowable.

Tima licks the candy like a puppy and looks up at her.

"Say thank you and put your hat back on; then the lady will give you another."

Tima freezes in disbelief.

"You can't get sick now—Granny Sima is coming home. Remember Granny Sima? She doesn't allow you to go out without a hat. Put it on, and the lady will give you another candy!"

The lady mumbles something about her ulcer and about her mommy, who makes her carry around imported candy everywhere. "He won't have a reaction to chocolate? My son does."

"Unfortunately, he may." We are not beggars!

"I only have chocolate left."

Tima's eyes shine like two diamonds. The tears will come in a second. But he turns away. He's ashamed of these tears; this is the beginning of pride. Head up, my little one. His hand finds mine, and he pinches it painfully.

The lady stuffs herself with chocolate.

"All right," I announce majestically. "Just this once. It's not real chocolate anyway—mostly soybeans."

Tima chews with his mouth open, like his great-grandmother.

They are expecting us at the camp. It's dark out. After the city, the clean country air intoxicates. Snowy dust swirls in the yellow light of the streetlamps.

"Do you want some tea?" they ask us. "The children have just had theirs."

I tell them no, thanks, we must get ready for the reading, but the bard interrupts me: Of course we'll have some tea; it's good for the voice!

We are sitting in an enormous dining hall. I'm drinking cup after cup of hot tea with candy and have already pounced on two huge slices of bread—they serve big, round loaves here. I love bread more than any delicacy. The room is warm, and my nose starts running. I carry a clean rag in my briefcase, but I'm ashamed to produce it here, so I take a piece of scrap paper that they use for napkins. I can hear the children's voices; they are being herded into the auditorium. Xenia and I quickly visit the bathroom, where she lifts her skirt and removes warm long johns. I glimpse her girdle. How often we forget our ugliness and present ourselves to the world au naturel, fat, flabby, unwashed. I'm sure her husband strays from her, repelled by the horror—for what's to like in an old person? Everything's bursting like an overripe orange; it's not spoiled, not yet—it's yesterday's good milk. In the east they'd wrap us in three layers and paint our hands and feet with henna.

I give my reading; the kids have quieted down. Tima is with me on the stage, as always, playing loudly with the water pitcher, slurping poisonous tap water—not his worst behavior. The teachers are poised behind the brats like overseers, oozing displeasure. In the end the art wins out, and I get my share of applause; Tima and I go to the wings to await our dinner. I want to send him down to the audience, to watch Xenia's performance—I need to collect my thoughts. But he climbs on my lap, jealous and demanding, and so we watch Xenia from behind. She pokes a large potato with a fork, arranges a bit of coarse fiber for hair, adds a ladle and thongs, and to my surprise performs a very original little skit. Even in our ancient bodies some intellect glimmers. Remember my great almost-namesake.

After the performance we celebrate in the dining hall. The children come over to look at the puppets, and I deftly drop into my briefcase three huge slices of buttered bread, plus some candy, for the evening feast at home. And then, with maximum flattery, I extract from Xenia a large potato, clearly bought at a private market—in order, I lie, to repeat the tale to Tima, but in fact for our second course. Alas.

Homeward. Morning awaits me, the morning of the final decision. The pension, the pension. But there is the smell to consider. Like in a zoo. Mama didn't make it to the bathroom, neither did her ward mates, and oh, how it stank in that ward. They were terribly ashamed, those grannies, and would pull up their covers, smearing themselves on the chin. In my presence a nurse pulled down the covers of Mama's neighbor, Krasnova, screaming at her, Look at yourself, you such and such, up to your neck, such and such. At that moment I saw in my mother's dull little eyes a glimmer of triumph. How well I knew that glimmer! How often I observed it through her ostensible pique—pique on my behalf—when she was defending me from my poor husband. The glimmer signified the triumph of her righteousness, of her right over my wrong. I honestly think that her few acts of kindness were performed out of spite—for me. Kindnesses are often performed in protest; the little one will befriend his so-called mother, my daughter, simply to protest against me and my righteousness, and whether for better or for worse I'm not sure.

Our bellies full (macaroni with ground beef, sweet tea, three slices of bread with butter—the children in our country have it good), we crawl home. Tima used to go to a day care, too. They would feed him, while I would catch up on sleep, go to the library, visit Burkin, and even concoct a very decent skirt out of scraps. But Tima was constantly sick. Every week of freedom cost me two months of his illness, when he would stay at home, pitiful and thin, and torment us both. What do they do to these children that they come home exhausted and full of aggression, and get sick as a result? Or is it the children who torment the other children? We lost our spot; there is a long wait-list to get in.

All night I churned on my sofa like on a hot plate, trying to decide. Then I glanced at the window and shuddered: something ugly and white clung to the glass, and I realized it was dawn. My judgment day had arrived. If my mother lived here with me, if I could endure that hell—the constant screaming, the insults—then I'd also have to deal with her paranoia about ambulances and policemen. We tried at first, idiots that we were, to convince her that the cop outside the supermarket was simply standing there (Andrey would work himself to a froth coming home from interrogations), and I begged her to believe me that the ambulance hadn't arrived for her, but then, of course, it did.

That's how matters stood. Alena wept herself into prostration every night; then she went into an eating frenzy, which drove Andrey mad. He always made sure everyone got their equal share of dessert; at the table he would torment little Alena by placing his unfinished cake in a prominent spot, like a sadist. Something has always been wrong in our family when it came to food. Poverty was to blame for all those petty reckonings, who ate how much of what; my mother constantly accused my husband of stealing food from his children. But I never accused anyone except for the dud, who did in fact deprive his child of nourishment, but that was later; that was a reaction to the shock I experienced when I found out everything, in a conversation with Veronica, Alena's classmate who also worked on the farm that fall. I called her to ask to talk to Alena, as her comrade, about her disturbing behavior, and she replied venomously that in a few months, when Alena felt better, she should take a moment to consider her future behavior with boys. (I was clueless! If I'd only read that diary earlier.) Veronica informed me that Alena and the boy were to be tried by the Komsomol court, but that she personally wasn't going to have anything to do with that charade; unlike my daughter she had refused to go with Shura to the hayloft, although Shura approached everyone in turn. It was disgusting to watch, but she never threw herself at him, because for her a cute face in a man is not the most important thing, that's right.

From this speech I drew the right conclusion, and for the next several weeks Veronica became my main ally. That was the month when Andrey came home from the interrogations and lay down facing the wall; when my mother sat in her room in the dark and ate almost nothing, and then one time, when I brought her food, she looked at me sideways, and I saw her eyes, bright red. What she knew, what she understood was hard to tell; everything happened quietly; we scurried around like mice, and Andrey disappeared into the maw of the investigation machine without a sound. I flew from the detective to the lawyer to meetings with Veronica, and Alena, now alone in her room, cried softly.

We—Veronica and I—never let the matter reach the Komsomol court. Veronica personally went to the administration to argue that Shura must marry

Alena at least temporarily, which suited me just fine, for what use could I have for that bastard. Veronica, meanwhile, enjoyed her new access to that secret idol of every girl in their class, who said little, and whose eyebrows, I must admit, were like a swallow's wings, and whose cracked mouth... Oh, mother's hatred for a son-in-law, it's jealousy and nothing more. My mother had always wanted to be the only object of my love and trust, wanted to be my entire family, to replace everything and everyone in my life. I've seen such families: mother, daughter, and small child. The daughter goes to work like a man; the mother stays home, nags the daughter that she comes home late, doesn't spend her money responsibly, doesn't pay enough attention to the child, and so on. At the same time the mother is insanely jealous of every girl-friend, let alone man, in whom she correctly sees a rival, and the result is one big mess. My own mother had pushed out my poor husband; in a good moment she looked at me slyly and asked, "So, who's the head of the family?"

On coming home one day I discovered Granny's door barricaded. When I pushed my way in, my mother was crouching in the dark on her little sofa (now it's mine). Why did you block the door? Why did you move the desk under the chandelier? Were you go-ing to hang yourself? When the paramedics arrived, she looked at me wildly, threw her head back, and walked out, for good. That night I howled and howled, and I couldn't stop. Alena shuffled in with some sedatives and doled out two pills, but I grabbed the whole bottle and asked her to bring me water; while she was gone, I stuffed the pills inside my pillow—I knew whom she was saving them for. You are hysterical, stop it, my daughter said, and what could I tell her? That I had come back from the hospital, with its barred windows? That Andrey has also been thrown behind bars? That I was a criminal? Who sends their mother to an institution? The doctors told me it was a very advanced schizophrenia—she herself told them about when the KGB began to follow her. I mentioned her scarlet eyes; they said it happens. She needs treatment, they said. Her life was in danger.

I knew, of course, that I couldn't bring Mama home—because of Tima: he didn't deserve that hell—the screams, the arguments, the smell, the feces. No pension would ever make up for all that, especially such a tiny one—she'll put a kettle on the stove and burn down the house. Tima came to me, and I greeted him with a smile as always, and promised him bread with butter from last night, and tea with candy, and to make him a house from paper. My head ached. I put water on for tea and thought I could just as easily forget to turn off the gas and burn down the house; that it was a miracle that all this time I had managed not to lose keys or money and to answer the letters coherently. But what if it happens before I leave for good—who will save Tima? There must always be other people in the house, but where are they? Where?

At this very moment the doorbell rang. Another friend of Andrey's? I've paid! I've paid everything I have, there's nothing left, leave me alone, you bastards! My hands were shaking: Who is it? I asked. The little one rushed to open the door—he opens to anyone, always.

"It's me, me."

"Who's me?"

"Me, Alena."

Why was she here? It wasn't her payment day! "It's Mommy!" Tima rejoiced for some reason.

I cracked open the door.

"What are you waiting for, Mama?" Her large eyes feigned curiosity. In her arms she was clutching a baby, her third, while her second was clutching at her skirt. My daughter was clad in a jacket two sizes too small, clearly from the trash. She was surrounded by a stroller, a sack, a suitcase. How did she manage to drag it all upstairs?

"We can't afford to receive you here, you hear me?"

I wanted to shut the door, but the little one wouldn't

let me. His mother was trying to unlock the door with her key; she addressed Tima through the crack: "Please, honey, step aside. She'll jam your finger with the door!"

"That's right, Timochka," I told him sweetly. "Let's close the door, sweetie." No!

I walked away and locked the door to my room. They scuttled past my door to the kitchen, then to the bathroom. I could hear Tima's happy voice, the baby singing, their mother cooing. He saved them; he is a member of their family now. For this I went hungry and sleepless, and at the first opportunity he tosses me aside like an old brick. In one brief instant my life has lost its meaning. How well he played his cards. A quick struggle at the door, and he is hers, his biological mother's. I've seen such cuckoo-mothers, who receive their children years later, and how those children adore them, how they instantly forget those who had raised them. I remember a very distant acquaintance, a certain Irina, telling me that now she knew why she could never get along with her mother: her mother wasn't her real mother! So now this Irina visits the grave of her real mother, which the fake mom had maintained all those years, while the woman who had fed and raised her gets nothing, even though Irina knows she's been ill and had to retire from her high post. Her husband Irina also kicked out, after a consultation with the grave, because he came from the same privileged milieu. Now she lives alone with a little daughter in a condo her fake mom bought for her. I remember mulling over this story because I also wanted my mother not to be my mother. I didn't understand then, and my heart went out to the grave of that birth mother, not to the adoptive mom, with her crew cut and ugly business jacket. I could imagine her with red cheeks and shaking hands breaking the news to Irina: she probably hoped for some gratitude at the end of her life, some justification of her sacrifices, and what did she get?

It was my turn to sit on the little sofa behind the locked door, my eyes bloodshot. Alena was going to move in here with her pack of brats. She'd take over the larger room, and Tima would move in with me, with his cot. I would celebrate my solitude at night, in the kitchen. There was no room for me here. When I came out, my eyes were dry.

"Alena, can I talk to you?"

"Wait, Mama. I'm unpacking. Can you feed Tima and Katya?"

Mama. A prick in the heart.

"Are you here for good? Is this it?"

"Tima, can you feed Katya? Grandma won't feed her."

"I can!" Tima yelped excitedly, and walked this fat Katya past me without a sign of recognition, as if I were a lamppost.

"There's nothing to eat, nothing!"

"Mommy," Tima announced, "we have two slices of bread with butter, and candy. I can put the water on."

"Alena, stop him, he'll burn himself and the little one. You'll have to watch him—I need to leave."

"You're leaving?" she said dully. Clearly she'd been hoping to leave me with the brats.

"That's right. Today I'm bringing home Granny," I announced.

She froze. "Mama! Why? Why today? Stop your jokes. There are three children here."

"Otherwise in an hour they'll transfer her to the facility for the chronically insane."

"So what?"

"What do you mean, so what? Who's going to visit her there? Take her food? They'll hit her over the head with a chair and that'll be it."

"You'll visit. Like you have done all these years. Or haven't you? You are getting her pension, after all."

"It's three hours one way!"

"You'll manage, for your own mother. You'll still be getting her pension."

"What pension? There will be no pension!"

"Ah, now I understand. Because of a few pennies we'll have to go through the same hell. My whole

94

childhood, all the best years ruined by screaming. Twisted family."

"Well, so that you can have a normal, untwisted family, Granny has disappeared."

"I've listened to these tales for years."

"To save you and your family, I sent her away, so your Shura could live with you here. But he couldn't! No one ever could!"

To my surprise her eyes filled with tears. A vestige of shame still dwelled in her.

"Don't cry, Mommy," Tima begged her.

"Sonny, where did you leave Katya? She can't be alone in the kitchen."

"Our Andrey is being kicked out by his wife, by the way. He drinks, you know."

Here I lied. One night Andrey pounded on my door screaming murder, and I caved and opened the door. There were three of them standing behind his back, hands in their pockets. I closed the door in their faces. Andrey was pale: he begged me on his knees—he owed eight hundred rubles. Under their watchful gazes I withdrew family savings, plus my mama's insurance—everything I had. He promised to give up drinking, to find work, to get treatment for his foot, and to register at his wife's address.

"Family, family," Alena sighed.

"Granny will sleep in the little room; I'll move

into the kitchen. If Andrey comes home, he'll sleep with Granny—he's her darling grandson."

"Andrey's no one's darling grandson, not anymore. I went to see him last night, with the children, and he threw a drunken fit in the middle of the night. They had a fight, turned on the lights—that was his way of telling us to get out."

"But he has promised to quit!"

"He's been drinking nonstop for a week—he found money somewhere. The house is full of his buddies. Well, at least this room is mine. Ours."

I'm choking on my tears. Andrey, Andrey. How could you? The decision came suddenly. Freedom! Wasn't it absurd to imagine freedom in such a space? Alena wouldn't be heartbroken. What abyss did she emerge from that a single room for four people she considered a refuge?

She read my mind. "I request political asylum. Mama! If you only knew how I lived!"

One moment of closeness between us in three years.

"Then why did you have another one? Why didn't you get rid of it?"

"Get rid—of Nikolai? Mama! How can you say that?"

"Everyone does it up until the last moment. Big deal. You pay money and have it done."

"Money? What money, Mama?" she mumbled.

"*Their* money. From *them*. The ones you spread your legs for. And you were taking from *us*! Whore."

I needed to hurry—they take them away early. They had already wrapped her in two robes, towel for a hat, rubber boots—in this cold! That's how they dressed her once for the X-rays—the machine is in a different building; I came to see her, saw an empty cot. What a scare I had! Why did they let me see it? Right now my mother's the last one left on the floor, her neighbor Krasnova's gone, everybody's gone, Mama receives special treatment as their only patient, and she greedily swallows additional food, her face contracting like a sponge. I won't survive, she whispers. Of course you will! the nurse tells her. What do you have to worry about, Granny? We'll take you to a new hospital; our beloved state won't abandon you—you'll always have your bowl of mush. Look at this sleeping beauty. Let's go, Granny, I'll rinse you off. Look at you—just skin and bones. The other day we lifted her neighbor, and she left her womb behind on the bed. Eighty-seven years old, they took her to the Fifth; the Fifth is much worse. You, Granny, they'll take to another dump; it's a bit cleaner. Who can find enough sheets and diapers for you, eh? Look at her, just like a baby. What is she saying? What are you saying, Granny? They should give them a shot and be done with it. Come, up you go.

But I must bring her some clothes. She's thin, she can wear mine. But mine are all unwashed or full of holes. At least she doesn't need a bra, and here's a pair of underpants saved for a doctor's visit, oh, happiness. Now. A slip. Nothing but holes. I mend now and again but not enough—no one sees me anyway. But what is this? Aha. An undershirt left by my former son-in-law, Shura. Thanks, Shura honey. I don't have tights for her, but here's a pair of sweatpants. Now I need socks without holes, but what's this? A pair of unworn cotton stockings. I'll roll them down, and she'll wear them like socks with her shoes.

God help me, what am I talking about? What shoes? It's winter, she'll need felt boots. I keep my pile of felt boots in storage. Oh, what a mess; how will I find anything in here? Idiot, lazy cow, all you care about is your stupid poetry, and now you are late and they are taking her away.

"Mama, don't make dust, for God's sake!" my daughter announces in passing.

I'm late, oh dear. Now her dress: thank God she's shorter than I am. I didn't touch anything, despite my intention to make something for myself out of different dresses. In the end I saved everything for Alena—she is the same height as my mother, has the same temper, too. Alena the Troglodyte, I called her to myself the last time she was here, when she shoveled two helpings of everything, but that was because she was heavily pregnant—I didn't know. Aha, here's something—a lovely tailored dress. Mama was an elegant young lady in a cutthroat all-female office, had lovers among the highest management, the bastards. The hat. The main thing is to cover your ears, I've been telling the little one. I was his doormat; he wiped off his silky feet and marched on—don't think, don't cry, he is fine, he is with his family, his mother, his brother and sister. The mother will shear his curls and put him up at a boarding preschool, like army service. A single mother is entitled to the state day care—prison for the children. She'll warehouse them all and go to work. But how is he going to sleep there alone? How? As your own mother has slept for almost seven years, that's how, but let's not think about that; let's think about finding a scarf for her. That would be with Tima's things; he wears it when his ears hurt, but it's covered with stains, with camphor oil—I can't put it on my mother's head!

Nothing, Alena dear, I'm not taking anything, just looking for a hat for Granny—she's completely bald, not a hair left. I'll give her my scarf; I'll raise my collar. Now I need a suitcase—it's on top of the wardrobe. Look at this dust; I'll wipe it with a rag. Now, clean sheets on the sofa, oh, and a rubber sheet underneath. Alena dear, you don't have an extra rubber sheet, do you? I didn't think so. I'll use a plastic bag, or better yet

I'll ask for an old one at the hospital. Now run, run, run, fifty-two times a year plus New Year's Eve, plus her birthday, plus Women's Day, plus the Revolution Day, before and after, because the chief psychiatrist Revekka Samoilovna, may she rest in peace, hinted once that on holidays patients cry and ask for sleeping pills and die. Revekka, we worshipped you like a deity, and who remembers you now? I do.

What a heavy suitcase, my God. Where am I going? It's one o'clock, they're all gone. The unheated ambulance has taken her to the dump to die. I'll get there and everything will be locked, no one will be around except the painters. Been ages since I've had my apartment painted. Young man, could you give up your seat? I'm going to faint; thank you, thank you. The train is barely crawling. How am I going to get her home? I've no money for a cab. Unless she's gone, as you are hoping in your lowly heart of hearts. I don't like the subway—tunnel noise scares me. They are looking at me, thinking, Where is this exhausted woman going with that suitcase? Remember your teeth; always smile with your lips closed. Young lady, please, could you give up your seat? I can barely stand; thank you. Let's go!

Run, run, run. At least her outfit's not completely shameful. Old people like old things. I forgot her ivory brooch! I'll give her my cardigan and will button it up. A long line for the shuttle. Please, people, let me go first: the psychiatric hospital is closing. That's right, I'm a patient there! Could you pass my fare to the driver? Double? Why? Oh, the suitcase. Shall we get going? The seats are all full.

No ambulance at the door. The steps. How my heart is pounding. I'm sorry for the knocking; I'm picking up my mother. I'm not too late, am I? Oh, thank God, I was so afraid I'd miss her. You see, my daughter showed up unexpectedly with her three children—the poor thing, she's completely alone, everyone's abandoned her. I saved my son, too. Some criminals threatened him; I paid them off. He worships me now, but he is an invalid with one heel. Is this her discharge form? Can I keep it, as a memento? What's your name, dear? Sonya? What a lovely name, very rare these days, a name from Dostoevsky. I was going to present you with a book of my poems—I'm a poet, you know. When it comes out I'll give every nurse a copy. In the meantime, Sonya dear, any equipment you may spare: a chamber pot, a rubber sheet, old sheets. I have absolutely nothing to put under her. Oh, thank you, thank you. Just throw everything into the suitcase; it'll be empty. Will you bring her out, or do I go right in? Hi, Mom, how are you? Let's get dressed. Want to go pee-pee for the road? Excellent. Look, Sonya, she understands everything! Sonya dear, what about her medications? A list of what she needs? Mama, we are getting dressed. What happened to her hair? Why did they shave her head? Look at her nails—did they never cut them? Oh, how my back hurts. Mama, look, wonderful Sonya brought us some pills for the next few days—I didn't dare to ask! Sonya, I'm dizzy; it's her smell, like a sick animal's. Please, could you find me a few drops of valerian? Now the boots, not very comfortable with those toenails, I know.

Mama, try to stand up straight. How will I take you home? Sonya, you mentioned an ambulance; can you ask them to just take us home? I don't have money for a cab—my book, you see, isn't out yet; when it comes out I'll pay everyone I owe.

"Look, Grandma," Sonya tells me reasonably, "if you're taking her home, the hospital isn't responsible for transportation."

"Sonya dear, as an exception, I beg you on my knees, please take us home. All the doctors are gone; there's no one else to beg. . . ."

"You must speak to the driver—that's up to him." And she scuttles away, having lost interest in our drama.

We are dressed and waiting. Mama is crouching on the bed; soon she'll pee herself. Loud banging on the stairs—a paramedic walks into the hall.

"Patient Serafima Golubeva!"

"She is here, I'm coming with her, I've got her papers. Please, young man, help her down the stairs."

Sonya is watching. As soon as we are on the stairs she locks the door inside. That's it.

My mother walks in a strange, jerky way. The paramedic supports her. Her shaved head is too small for my hat.

We are inside the ambulance.

"Excuse me, which way are we going?"

"The Fifth."

"The Fifth? We were told the other one. How far is the Fifth?"

"Three hours one way, then back to the city, to the depot."

"Here's my offer. You can drive us for three hours, in the cold. Or it can be a quick twenty-minute drive."

"Where's that?"

"Home. I'll sign a paper that I changed my mind and took her home. At five you'll be off."

"Ah, you old . . . If you are taking her home, call the cab. Get out now, both of you."

"No, I won't get out. We will go straight to the Fifth, and there the chief will order you to take her home. Let's go."

"Hand over her papers."

"No. I'll give you her papers when we get to my

house. Come on, it's easier for everyone this way. What am I to do? She can't walk—she can't!"

"We have paperwork for the Fifth; they'll sign it there."

"Fine, let's go to the Fifth, but they'll send you back, I guarantee. Six hours in this cold. Just tell them at the depot that the patient was taken home, so you wasted a ride."

"We know what to say."

"And I'll give you her paperwork. Please, think about it—look at the weather; she may die on you!"

"That's it, get out. We are going to the depot."

"No, you will go with us."

"Look at yourself. You yourself should be committed, you old . . ."

I'm shaking, but the valerian drops are doing their job. With energy and calm I'm drilling holes in the drivers' dim brains. They understand (I imagine their thought process) that something's not right, that I'm trying to trick them. On the other hand, if they get rid of me quickly, they can get a nice, easy assignment: a family hacked to pieces by a drunken husband, for example.

"I sympathize, I do, but you won't get rid of me. I have her paperwork. In a moment she'll take a dump all over your floor."

My old girl mumbles something from her cot. The drivers are glaring at us hatefully.

"Just take us home, I beg you. It's half an hour."

The driver starts the car reluctantly. I yell out the address, but they can't hear it. Where are they taking us? I can't see through the whitewashed windows; they whitewash the windows, so as not to upset the public. No one should see what takes place inside—the strait-jacket, the final horror, the death. Paramedics are the ultimate power; they know neither weakness nor mercy.

After ten minutes they stop. But where are we? How did we get here?

"Please, are you sure we're at the right entrance? I understand no one will help me get her out, and I would have taken a cab, but the pension, you see, is only two days from now. Please, where are we?"

"Get out."

I drop my suitcase in the snow, then drag out my mother, who is weightless but unwieldy. The two men are sitting in the front cabin, smoking. As soon as I close the door, the ambulance scurries away, like an overfed bug.

We are standing on a bridge at the end of a gray winter day. In every direction I see factory pipes; under the bridge run railroad tracks. A streetcar rolls past, muffled by snow. I don't recognize anything. Those paramedics have seen it before—clever relatives like me, who try to save their parents and children from the miserable end; they know how to deal with us.

We are shivering on the sidewalk. I had sat my mother down on the suitcase; suddenly she jerks, then droops again. I know she's peed into her boots. Right now she's warm; soon she'll freeze. I grab her with one arm, wrestle the suitcase with the other, and drag her through the snow along the streetcar tracks in the direction of the stop. Someone will help us, I tell myself; the streetcar's warm, and it will take us to civilization.

There is a noise behind us. I look around, through the thickening blizzard, and see an ambulance. Thank God, some kind soul called for it. A man opens the door: it's him, the paramedic. They came back. He lifts my mother and tosses her onto the cot. It's warm inside. He covers her with a blanket. Her head sinks into a white pillow; I see her caved mouth and the slits of her eyes. Her face is wet with melting snow.

"Sign it," and he shoves a piece of paper at me.

That's why he came back. Everything needs to be signed.

At home Alena is waiting—the children. How can I bring this filth, this old body, into that sacred nursery? Why did I terrorize poor Alena all day? I myself should leave.

The paramedic takes the signed paper and climbs back into the ambulance to arrange my mother on the cot. He looks back at me, waiting for me to say good-bye, but I can't move. Then he comes out, slams the door, and climbs into the front seat, then slams that door, too, and the heavy vehicle sets off.

Into the nearest garbage can I unload my suitcase. I keep only a ball of cotton. Now Alena will drop all three on my back, but I'll need to find time to visit Mama. Why didn't I wipe her face? I was frozen on the spot—over what? Big deal—a sack of old bones is dragged to an almshouse. They must do it a hundred times a day. Why weep on the subway? It's the law of nature: the old must make room for the young.

I reach my sacred hearth and tiptoe into my room. The apartment smells of babies and burnt milk. In the kitchen the refrigerator is rumbling like an empty stomach. I peel off my wet clothes, take a warm bath, lie down on my bed, and wake up, as always, at midnight.

The time is night. I'm alone in the kitchen. This is my time of peace, of conversation with deity and stars. Everything is quiet, the fridge has been turned off, but from afar comes the blood-chilling sound: Niura pounding bones for tomorrow's soup. How many times we've asked her not to do it at night. But why so quiet? Three children didn't make a peep all night? Their mother not once visited the kitchen to heat up the milk? Everyone must be tired. But living children don't sleep like that! What has she done? Stop imagining things. Niura must have lost her marbles. She can't feed her children, so she finds soup bones somewhere and pounds them into jelly, then boils them. Good for her. But I can't go there. Four coffins, one smaller than the other, and flowers. How to dig up the graves in the middle of the winter? Andrey would get drunk. The dud wouldn't have the guts to show up.

The pills, she always kept pills. But why take the children? The baby probably needed just a crumb in a drop of milk. The dead always look so relieved, as if they've just had a good cry. How long is she going to pound those bones? She'll tell me to fuck off, a hard-working woman. Everyone is used to the noise and sleeps right through it.

I do two things. First, I knock on Niura's door. When she opens it, all sweaty from her pounding, I explain to her in the language she can understand that if she doesn't stop her racket I'll report her son for vandalizing pay phones. When she opens her mouth, I slam the door in her face. Next, I march into my daughter's room. It's empty. There's no trace of them— only a squashed pacifier on the floor. She took them away, all three. Where? Doesn't matter. The main thing is they are alive. All the living have left me. Alena, Tima, Katya, even the tiny Nikolai. Serafima. Anna. Forgive my tears.

Chocolates with Liqueur

1

The Housing Question

Nikita left his wife, Lelia, but for the time being he let her and their children stay in their two-room apartment.

He didn't mention divorce.

Every night he came at seven and stayed in "his" room for two hours, watching television or talking very loudly on the phone.

The children were forced to sleep in these conditions. But they got used to the noise and to the idea that Papa was not to be disturbed.

He and Lelia agreed that he wouldn't get there before seven. From seven to nine was his time.

Occasionally, the upstairs neighbor took in the children for those two hours.

To the children Lelia explained the arrangement

as "Papa is working." There wasn't any need to explain anything, but Lelia tried at all costs to keep up an appearance of a normal family. The children, she thought, must not suffer—they must have a father.

In Nikita's presence, Lelia made no demands, didn't ask for anything, barely lifted eyes at him. Yes, no, as you wish. Even when she was in bed with a high fever and there was nothing to eat in the house, she said nothing when Nikita arrived at his usual time and turned on the TV particularly loudly. She was calm, with the serenity of someone who has hit bottom.

She and the children had nothing to live on. Nikita paid only for the utilities (having installed the weakest bulbs), and Lelia, a nurse, couldn't work: her little daughter was constantly sick.

Lelia came from an educated family. After her father died, her mother took up drinking and, for some reason, sold their apartment. She bought a room in a communal apartment—to live in while she looked for another place—and that's where they stayed. The money quickly ran out.

When Lelia was away at summer camp, her mother remarried. Her new husband was an out-of-town vendor who sold fruit at an outdoor market and rented a room in the same communal apartment. The mother registered him in their room—and his numerous relatives from his home village—and almost immediately died. All this happened within just two weeks.

When the poor girl arrived home from camp, she found the room where she had lived with her mother packed floor to ceiling with dark-skinned people who replied to all her questions with "no speak Russian."

Later the fruit seller took her to see her mother's grave and showed her all the papers. Everything was in order.

Lelia went to her only remaining relative, her grandfather, who lived in Sergiev Posad, forty miles from the city. Her grandfather went to the police, but they only shrugged: Lelia's mother was an alcoholic. They advised Lelia to hire a lawyer—but with what money?

There was nothing to do but register Lelia at Sergiev Posad, where her grandfather owned half of a house with an orchard.

Lelia quit school and began training to be a nurse. As soon as she graduated and started her first job at a large hospital, her grandfather died of a heart attack.

Immediately, the owner of the other half of the house, her grandfather's niece by marriage, tried to lay her hands on Lelia's property—but the grandfather had arranged things well and the niece got nowhere. For consolation, she moved the fence in the orchard, annexing all the gooseberry and black currant bushes. In order to sue her, Lelia had to show a deed to the house, but it miraculously disappeared during the wake, which the niece attended.

Such was Lelia's life story.

One night Lelia asked her husband, Nikita, if she could rent his room for three months to some female students.

"Maybe *I* will rent *my* room to fruit sellers from the market. How about it? Look at this mistress of the house! The apartment is mine, and I can do what I want with it."

"As you wish."

Everything had been said between them. After one terrible scene Nikita announced he would no longer give them a penny beyond utilities, and he kept his word. One more time, like a broken record, Lelia asked him to divide their apartment—or else she'd take the matter to court. Lelia knew that only the threat of legal action would have some effect on Nikita; but he knew, in turn, Lelia's timid and inert nature and that she'd never be the first one to file for divorce. He just swore at her and slammed the door.

Lelia perched on a stool in the kitchen, catching her breath. Something was seriously wrong with Nikita; he looked awful. What was he planning? To hire a killer to get rid of them? He didn't have the money. His mother and sister would never sponsor him. And why wasn't he eating or drinking at their house? Maybe he didn't want to take the last crumbs from his undernourished children? That had never stopped him in the past.

That Nikita was mentally ill Lelia had known for some time. There was plenty of evidence: changes in his appearance, sudden rages, ridiculous suspicions. He found a new pair of scissors and decided that Lelia was turning tricks for money; he stayed late, waiting for her lovers to show up.

What he didn't know was that for two whole months Lelia had been working. In the face of mortal fear and shyness, she plastered their neighborhood with handwritten ads for a home playgroup, every day from ten to five. Some days there would be seven children, plus Lelia's two—a handful.

Every day, rain or shine, Lelia took her brood to the park and kept them there for two hours. At home, after lunch, they drew, and Lelia taught them a little English. At five, the parents took them home. Lelia's own children felt perfectly at ease among them.

Lelia's firm rule was that children had to be picked up by five. If a parent was late, she took the child home and charged for an extra full day.

Nikita couldn't know about the playgroup—there was no telling what a demented person might do.

Lelia's children, Anya and Gleb, quickly got used

to the new regimen. In the fridge there was a container labeled "Teatime" with candy and crackers for the group, and the children knew not to touch it. Even though Lelia still lived in constant tension, things improved a little.

Day in, day out, a string of children crossed through a tunnel and emerged in the park on the other side. There was a slide, a merry-go-round, and a gazebo in which to take shelter from rain. Ilya liked to fight and always had a runny nose. Methodius, an angel with flaxen curls, wept for hours on end. Kirill was dragged to the park an hour late, and Lelia ended up carrying around his lunch pail. His lunch always consisted of condensed soup and tinned fish; tea with sugar was a special treat for him.

At half past four they had tea with crackers from the container in the fridge: children adore other people's food. Anya and Gleb assisted Lelia during lunch and teatime, and the other children always closed their pails neatly and put them away.

They even had a New Year's pageant. Lelia taught the children some English nursery rhymes, and they recited "Little Mouse, Little Mouse" before their parents and grandparents. The kids were wearing costumes with masks and white tights; their parents brought their presents from home and placed them under the tree.

Only poor Kirill didn't have a present—his harassed mom dropped him off at the last minute and ran home. Gleb found him a pair of white tights, and Kirill brilliantly played the part of Mouse (such semi-neglected children from educated families often grow up to become real talents). He received a hastily compiled present: a few caramels and tangerines. He couldn't believe his happiness and immediately began munching.

The children walked around the tree in a slow circle dance and sang; the parents and grandparents were touched to the point of tears. At the end they played parlor games. And at five sharp, mothers and grandmothers quickly rearranged the room, swept the floor, and promptly left. Kirill was taken home by a stern-looking big brother of seven. (In that family there were at least three other brats.)

At seven thirty Nikita staggered in. His eyes were bulging. His forehead was paper white; the rest of his face was scarlet. The children, who were resting on the couch in front of the TV, jumped up and made for the door, but Nikita stopped them. From his shabby briefcase he pulled out a box of chocolates—a present. Anya took the box timidly and placed it on the table.

"Eat," Nikita ordered.

Gleb swallowed one chocolate; Anya took one, too.

"You too, madam," Nikita said to Lelia. "Your favorite—with liqueur. Stuff yourself; don't be shy."

"Oh, but why do you give them liqueur?"

"Let them practice—their granny, after all, was an alcoholic. And their mommy's a whore," he added with pleasure.

"Thanks for the compliment, but I'm not hungry."

"I know you'll gobble everything down the moment I leave!"

But first he made sure the children ate two more chocolates. Eight remained in the box.

As soon as Nikita left, Lelia carried the children to the bathroom, made them drink a liter of water, and then induced them to vomit. After that she gave them warm milk. Then she put them to bed. The children were pale; their pulses were weak; they needed intravenous treatment urgently.

Lelia put the remaining chocolates in a plastic bag and hid them under the tub. She was collecting papers for hospitalization when Nikita thumped in with his heavy winter boots—Lelia barely had time to fall on the couch and close her eyes. When Nikita leaned over her and felt her pulse with his icy fingers, she opened her eyes and gave out a moan. Nikita jumped.

"Oh dear," Lelia moaned, "it hurts! I think I have the flu."

"And the children?"

"Long asleep."

He tiptoed to check, then asked, "Why so early?"

"We had some children over for the New Year; everyone ate too much and got overexcited. . . ."

"Ate too much? Where did you get the money to buy all that food?"

He rummaged in the kitchen, looking for something; he must have found the empty box.

"I see you really liked my chocolates."

"There were just a few left," Lelia moaned.

"Right. I have to go now. Be back soon."

Lelia jumped out of bed and tried the phone. There was no dial tone; he must have cut the cord.

The children were still breathing. Lelia had pumped their stomachs thoroughly, and the milk must have helped. But what's next? She couldn't call the ambulance. Was that his plan—to wait until they died from poisoning and then walk in with the police to remove the bodies? He looked completely demented.

Lelia closed the curtains, gathered their papers and money (the parents had just paid for the month), packed everything into an old backpack, and woke up the children. They were extremely weak. Lelia removed the poisonous chocolates from under the tub: they were beginning to melt; the poison was leaking. She quickly put on surgical gloves, wrapped the chocolates in some candy wrappers from the trash can, and put them in the "Teatime" container, which she shoved in the freezer.

The children got dressed and were standing shivering. It was past midnight.

Suddenly the lock creaked, and again Nikita staggered in. "What's wrong?" He seemed genuinely shocked to see them.

Hiccuping with fear, Lelia told him that they felt sick and needed to get to the hospital; they couldn't call the ambulance because the phone wasn't working. He walked them downstairs, flagged down a random car, gave the driver some cash, and told him to take them to the Thirty-Third Hospital. He walked around the car, memorizing the license plate.

The Thirty-Third was notorious for its inhumane treatment of the bums and homeless.

At the hospital Lelia got out, thanked the driver, immediately found another car, and asked to be taken to the Children's Hospital. There she explained that the children seemed to have been poisoned by some bad candy. She gave different names and promised to bring their IDs in the morning.

The children were so weak they couldn't talk.

She sat the night out at the waiting room; there was nowhere else to go.

In the morning she was told her children had been

poisoned by some untraceable substance and that it had affected their hearts.

They were in the ICU. Lelia immediately went to human resources. They didn't have a vacancy for a nurse; Lelia was hired as a janitor, to wash miles of floors, plus the toilets. No one else wanted to do the job for the money they paid. But at least she could see the children. They were almost invisible under the covers, but they were still alive.

In the evening Lelia went to check on her home. The lights were on; from the stairs she could hear Nikita talking to a woman.

"Imagine how much renovations will cost!" he was complaining.

"A terrible dump," the woman confirmed in a fat, confident voice. "How can one consider herself a mother and live in such conditions?"

"Forget it, it's over," Nikita responded. "I'll go to the hospital to make sure they are gone."

2

Rivals

Sometimes instinct compels a young man to pursue his prey, especially if there is a rival panting next to him, nose to nose. That's how they felt, those idle young men, the convalescing surgical patients at a large Moscow hospital. Their prey was a very young nurse, a real angel in white, Lelia, with soft, gentle hands and a sweet smile—an ideal wife.

Nikita was recovering from an appendectomy. After one look at Lelia he knew what he wanted. Compared to Lelia, he said to anyone who listened, proud city ladies were just overeducated whores with tiny salaries. Lelia even made her own clothes! She looked like a heroine from an American hospital drama: a little makeup, kitten heels, and a thick braid under her green cap. She came from an educated family and knew foreign languages.

Unfortunately for Nikita, there was another suitor, a certain Danila, who used to work at the hospital and was now back as a patient. He showed up every time Lelia was on duty and took her home. Every time he brought her chocolate—Nikita and the other patients already knew that Lelia loved chocolate. Nikita asked his sister to buy him the biggest and most expensive box, which he handed to Lelia one night during her shift. That shift he wouldn't leave her alone; they ended up talking all night. In the morning, however, Danila ran in panting, complaining about traffic—so he owned a car.

By profession young Nikita was a biochemist. That night he bragged to Lelia about inventing a perfect poison that doesn't leave a trace—people simply die from a heart attack. Nikita, it's true, seemed a little loopy: he was taking some self-made pills, supposedly for pain, and wouldn't shut up about his brilliant future, when he would have a beach mansion, a car, and six children. In the meantime, all he had to his name was a Moscow registration: he was registered at his grandmother's two-room apartment; the grandmother was bedridden, in the full throes of dementia; his mother and sister were taking care of her.

To all this Lelia replied that she didn't plan on

getting married just yet; that first she wanted to study, but of course medical school cost money, and even with her own vegetable patch and overtime at the hospital she couldn't afford it. Since her grandfather's death, Lelia had lived alone in his half of the house. Little by little she told Nikita everything.

"Well," Nikita announced. "True, we have nowhere to live just yet, but we already have a summer house. You are a bride with a dowry." As if everything had been decided!

Nikita found out that Danila was married to a woman seven years older with a child of her own.

A day after Nikita was discharged, he turned up during Lelia's night shift. He was very excited, his pupils dilated. He handed her a box of chocolates and announced that tomorrow morning they were going to apply for a marriage license. Then they would rent a room in the city to save Lelia her ninety-minute commute.

"As you wish," Lelia responded with a sweet smile. No more "I'm too young," "I want to study." Lelia never contradicted anyone, but did as she saw fit.

"Let me see your passport," Nikita demanded. "I want to make sure you are not married." Smiling sweetly, Lelia took out her passport from her locker and gave it to Nikita, who opened it, closed it, and put it in his pocket. Just like that.

In the morning Danila arrived and walked straight into the surgery, where Nikita told him to go back where he came from. "Let's step out and talk it over," offered burly Danila. But at this point the chief nurse interfered and asked Danila to leave—he was no longer their patient. "What about him?" roared Danila. "He came to remove his stitches. . . ."

The stitches were removed the previous night during Lelia's shift. That night Nikita, for the first time in his life, raped a woman. Lelia was afraid to call for help—he came to see her secretly, unofficially—and only cried and tried to avoid his kisses when he was forcing her painfully on the floor. As soon as he was done she ran away.

As Nikita later admitted, that night he experienced the full spectrum of emotions: passion, rage at the victim's resistance, pleasure, pride from the conquest, even anxiety for her—the girl, he said, was completely unprepared and fought back desperately, so he had to forget about caresses and just hammer his way in.

Danila waited outside in vain: Lelia and Nikita left through the basement door and took the train to Sergiev Posad.

Nikita spent two days in bed with Lelia in her house, which was clean but modest beyond his imagination: a brick oven in the room and the kitchen, handwoven runners on the floor, water in the buckets (brought from the outside well). The only object of value was an oak bookcase containing classics in Russian, French, and English.

The next day they took the train to Moscow and applied for a marriage license. Lelia submitted completely to Nikita's orders. She was mortally scared of him. For his part, Nikita seemed terrified of his mother and sister and didn't tell them about the impending wedding.

Three months later they got married.

It was summer. Nikita lived at Lelia's like at a resort. They had their own young potatoes, lettuce, parsley. Lelia didn't tell Nikita about her pregnancy.

After reading a manual, Nikita built a hothouse in the orchard. He and Lelia were proud that no one helped them. Nikita commuted to Moscow three times a week. He came back exhausted, physically and emotionally: mother and sister were nagging at him that he didn't help to care for his grandmother, and every time made him work on her bedsores, ostensibly because he knew biology. Once he cried out in exasperation that he wished his grandmother's apartment might rot in hell, he didn't care.

Lelia offered her services, but Nikita snapped at her that she shouldn't get involved. She knew then that he hadn't told his relatives about her.

As for Lelia's aunt, the owner of the other half of the building, she clearly was afraid of Nikita, who had promptly moved the fence back where it used to be and even a little farther out.

Now they had wonderful black currant, cultivated by Lelia's aunt over the years.

3

Family Life

Although Nikita refused to introduce Lelia to his mother and sister, he was extremely jealous of her and didn't want to leave her alone in the house. He thought he saw Danila on the platform once when he was waiting for the Moscow train. He stopped telling Lelia about his schedule at college, because he didn't want her to have trysts in his absence.

Next, his inflamed brain focused on her work at the hospital. More chocolate from patients? Why don't you bring it home? Without explanation he demanded that she switch hospitals, but Lelia explained calmly that it wouldn't be easy: she was in her fourth month of pregnancy.

Nikita almost fainted. "When did this happen? What about an abortion? How will we live through the winter with a baby? Mother and sister will fly off the handle!"

Lelia was arranging green tomatoes on the windowsill. She didn't say a word.

Nikita left, seemingly for good. Lelia didn't look for him. At the hospital she now had to work additional shifts for the two nurses on vacation. She didn't complain but looked so exhausted that Nadya, the chief nurse, prescribed her free vitamin shots. Lelia was certain that her husband had left her, but a week later he reappeared at the hospital at the end of her shift.

"Grandma died, had to bury her, this and that," was all he said.

He looked awful: his was the face of a murderer. He couldn't look Lelia in the eye. He spent two days by himself, on the cot behind the oven, getting up only to use the outhouse or to have a sip of vodka from his briefcase.

Lelia left for work; when she came back the nest was empty again. Three days later Nikita returned without a word of explanation. Again, he stayed in bed drinking.

Lelia was too scared to ask what was happening to him. Those days he attacked her without warning, felled her to the floor, and raped her, like the first time at the hospital. Lelia knew it was a perversion that wasn't going to change, and always tried to leave the room facing him, which irritated him beyond words. "Why do you keep curtsying to me? What are you, a slave?"

Some nights he would twist her braid around his arm, pull her up, and stare at her face. Lelia always closed her eyes.

"Why aren't you looking at me?"

Silence.

"Every female is a predator who consumes the male after she gives birth. That's what you are doing to me, understand? Consuming me."

As it grew colder, there was more work to be done around the house: someone had to chop fire-wood, but Nikita refused to lift a finger. Lelia continued to live as if she were alone: chopping wood, feeding the furnace twice a day, carrying water from the well, washing, cleaning, cooking.

On her payday she bought, as she had done in the past, some cheap pork from the neighbor (in exchange for administering him shots), and cured it in jars for the winter. Lelia was constantly hungry; she was so thin her pregnancy still didn't show.

Nikita gobbled down all that meat in a month. He couldn't stuff himself enough, and kept asking for more. From all that food, he gained weight and stopped attacking Lelia; now he did his business quietly in bed. He seemed to calm down somewhat but still didn't give her a penny.

Lelia didn't ask. She lived off her preserves, pickled cabbage and potatoes. At the hospital cafeteria she asked for leftover bread—presumably for a pig she kept. All she lacked was meat.

Then one night Nikita said, "Well, there's no crying over spilled milk. Pack your rags, we are moving to Moscow."

"But where in Moscow?"

"I've got Grandma's place, haven't I?"

In the late grandmother's lair the stench was indescribable. Every pipe leaked; the ceiling in the kitchen was black with soot. Most of the furniture had been taken out; what was left was broken, unusable.

4

Renovation

Between shifts Lelia scrubbed the place and primed it for painting. At the hospital she spoke to the painters who worked on the second floor, and they promised her plaster and paint. She asked Nikita to help her transport the heavy buckets, but he refused vehemently and again attacked her.

So Lelia called Danila and asked him to come to the hospital. Danila saw her belly and stopped in his tracks. They loaded supplies into his old car and drove to Lelia's apartment. There Danila moved all the furniture to the center of the room, after which Lelia ordered him to leave. Before leaving he kissed the hem of her robe. He seemed about to cry. Thank you, he whispered. Everyone knew how much he respected and feared his older wife.

Lelia worked quickly. She peeled the old wallpaper

and washed all the ceilings, walls, and windows. While the ceilings dried, she quickly painted the doors and window frames. In the evening Nikita came home, drunk. He yelled that she'd messed up his apartment, kicked the chair, and left.

Lelia had plastered the walls with old newspapers, but now she needed wallpaper. She took a bottle of medical spirits to the hospital painters, but they couldn't help her—they used only paint.

So she had to call Danila again, and ask him for money. They went together to an outdoor market, and chose wallpaper; Danila also bought her some paint for the kitchen.

Lelia treated Danila as if he were her husband, and in a sense he was.

He used to work on Lelia's hospital floor. Later he transferred to a different hospital, but when it turned out he needed surgery, he came back to his old workplace—he didn't want to convalesce among his own patients. His old colleagues adored him; as for Lelia, she practically worshipped him. He was everything to her: friend, adviser, and longtime lover.

She hoped that the baby that was growing inside her was his.

Danila helped her carry the wallpaper and paint to Nikita's apartment. They had tea. Lelia didn't cry.

In the evening the gloomy Nikita interrogated

her about the origins of the wallpaper. Lelia explained that the hospital painters exchanged it for a bottle of spirits. "But I can't hang it myself," she added. "Then fuck off," and he marched into the kitchen, where he saw a pot of unpeeled boiled potatoes.

"What's that supposed to be—my dinner?" he yelled, and hurled the pot onto the floor.

Quickly, before he hit her, Lelia picked up the potatoes and fried them with onion and a couple of carrots. Nikita was eating sardines straight from the can, for an appetizer. "The husband," he lectured her, slightly mollified, "must be greeted with a hot dinner and a full glass."

Then he gobbled down a jar of pickled cucumbers and a pan of fried potatoes. He announced that his sister and mother wanted to pay a visit. "But first you must finish putting up the wallpaper—I can't invite them to a hovel."

In the morning, after Nikita left, Lelia called Nadya, the chief nurse, and Raya, one of the cafeteria workers. By eleven at night they had papered both rooms. Lelia made them potatoes with salted pork, and Raya ran to the store for a bottle.

At eleven thirty Nikita arrived. "And who is this?"

"Don't you recognize them? Our chief nurse and Raya from the kitchen." Toothless Raya opened her arms to hug him. "My goodness, patient, come sit with us."

He sat down and ate and drank everything, then they showed him the rooms. Nikita couldn't believe his eyes. For the hall, they explained, they didn't have enough paper.

"Can't you ask the painters for more?" he asked.

"What painters?" Raya asked.

"The painters on your second floor."

"Ah, those," Nadya jumped in. "They already left."

Raya began to sing.

As soon as the women left, Nikita interrogated Lelia to the third degree, aiming for the belly. Lelia kept saying that she didn't have enough to live on, that he needed to chip in—there wasn't enough for food. Nikita screamed that she took money from lovers. The conversation ended, as always, on the floor.

When Nikita fell asleep, Lelia packed her things and went to the hospital. There she changed and lay down on the cot in the nurses' room—her shift began at nine in the morning. The next day she was on her way to Sergiev Posad, with Danila.

As a precaution she allowed him to take her only as far as the train station. From there she took the train to her unheated nest. Going through the familiar motions, she stoked the furnace, made herself some soup, and fell asleep until the next morning. She woke up from the bitter cold, fed the furnace again, and so on. She would have stayed there, but Nikita's demon couldn't leave her alone.

As she explained to Danila, Nikita needed a slave who would cost him nothing and whom he could kick whenever he wanted. "I can't leave him, do you understand? He'll kill me and the child; he already suspects the child isn't his."

Nikita showed up at the hospital at the end of Lelia's shift, and made her come back with him to the apartment.

Lelia saw the filthy hall and bathroom and announced that she was leaving—she'd had enough of his beatings.

"Ha! You haven't seen any beatings yet," Nikita promised her, beaming, and proceeded to take her on the dirty floor.

When he was done, Nikita opened the closet and showed her rolls of wallpaper—for the unfinished hall.

"Alone I can't."

Nikita softened. "I'll give you a hand—Mom and Sis are threatening to come."

Together they hung the paper, helter-skelter. Only then Lelia caught a quick nap.

In the evening there was a long ring on the doorbell, and Nikita opened the door to two massive ladies in furs. The ladies threw a glance at poor, swollen Lelia, then took a tour of the apartment.

Mother: "My God, where did you find such wallpaper? Like at Aunt Tosya's in the village."

Sister: "I'd be ashamed to live like this."

Mother: "Nikita, it's time you started making some money."

Sister: "I'll find him a job!"

Nikita: "Bartending?"

Sister: "And why not?"

Nikita: "Because I'm working on a thesis! Because I'm a research fellow!"

Sister: "Junior research fellow."

Nikita: "You've never made it this far, fucking speculator."

Mother, screaming: "Enough, I said!"

Sister, hysterically: "I'll never, ever accept a glass of water from him! On my deathbed I won't." This tirade she addressed to Mom: clearly, there was a history of great jealousy here; Mommy must have favored her little boy over this hog of a daughter.

They sat down to eat. In Lelia's opinion the food was fit for kings: salads, meatballs, fried potatoes, pickled mushrooms, and cucumbers.

Nikita swallowed mouthfuls, but he was the only one. The ladies declared that they had eaten, but Nikita didn't take offense. "You keep picking on me," he told them, chewing, "while I have developed the most effective, untraceable weapon!"

"Then you have to seek out the bandits; they are your buyers," instructed the sister.

"Put me in touch, then. Aren't you one of them?"

"Sure I will," the sister brayed merrily. "For three grand!" Nikita brayed along.

Six weeks later Gleb was born.

At the hospital gate Lelia was greeted by Nadya, Nikita, his mom, and his sister. The mother took one look at the baby and whispered something to the daughter. "That's right," the daughter agreed, "definitely not ours."

With a crooked smile Nikita took the baby and climbed into the cab. His ladies took a different car.

At home, surrounded by her new relations, Lelia changed the baby. He opened one eye and yawned.

"Oh, my sweetie pie," Nikita said happily. "Just look at him! He's just like me in that old picture." And he looked at his family expectantly. The double-headed monster—his mother and sister—pursed its lips meaningfully.

A year after the birth of the girl—whom Nikita's mother and sister didn't accept, either—Nikita left for another woman. Lelia's upstairs neighbor and friend, Tamilla, saw him once with a tall woman from the next building.

5

Dessert

Lelia was hiding on the stairs above her floor.

Her husband's lady friend continued with her reprimand.

"How can one live in such conditions, like a beggar, and call oneself a mother? How could you trust her with your children?"

"They are not my children," replied Nikita.

"You can't be too sure. You must take the test."

They disappeared into the elevator. Lelia waited another five minutes, then tiptoed into her apartment. First thing first: take the poisoned chocolates to her hospital lab.

Stunned, Lelia stared at the empty "Teatime" container. So he knows. He knows that all the chocolates weren't eaten and that his family is alive and hiding somewhere. Good thing she hadn't gone to Sergiev, where it's easy to stage a fire. She must remember to ask their local electrician to replace the old wires.

Lelia caught herself thinking like a criminal. What could she expect, after living for seven years with someone like him? Thank God the children weren't his.

With shaking fingers she packed some clothes and quietly left the house. She walked up to the next floor and pressed Tamilla's bell. Occasionally Lelia took in her eight-year-old son; Tamilla didn't want him to be home alone after school, even though they had a magnificent German shepherd, Jerry.

Lelia refused the offer of tea and asked if Tamilla was taking Jerry for a walk—she was afraid to walk alone in the dark and needed to administer a shot to a neighbor.

"Look at yourself," sighed Tamilla. "All you do is work, work, work.... You look like a war victim. There's a decent secondhand store nearby—go and buy yourself something."

"You are so right, dear! Thank goodness, it's vacation week. As for thinness, it's just my old friend gastritis," Lelia managed to joke.

Tamilla got dressed and leashed the shepherd. Jerry was a truly frightening beast who attacked other dogs without warning. But he adored Lelia and her children.

The courtyard was empty. Lelia took the bus to the Children's Hospital, where she spent the evening in the waiting room. All night she slept on the cot in the procedural room, which wasn't used after hours. By then, she had learned every nook in that hospital.

Ten days later, the children were discharged.

Pale and thin, they looked like little bums in their wrinkled clothes and shapeless shoes, which Lelia had stored in the hospital locker. There was nothing to do but travel to Sergiev, to the unheated house. But then Lelia thought, Why so far? If he wants to finish them off, he'll come to Sergiev; that will be even easier. So what's the difference? And so she took the children home, maybe for the last time.

In the elevator she lost her nerve and pressed Tamilla's floor. No one was home, to her horror; only the dog was clawing at the door, greeting the children. Gleb and Anya waited listlessly; they didn't even have the energy to greet Jerry.

Again, Lelia didn't have the nerve to take them home and instead left them at the playground in the courtyard. Under Tamilla's mat she left a note, asking her to pick up the kids on her way home from work and saying Lelia would get them in the evening.

With trembling fingers she unlocked her door. Familiar smells hit her in the face. But that was all that remained of her home.

Everything—every closet, shelf, and drawer—had been turned inside out, the contents spilled on the floor. In the middle of the kitchen stood a dirty cardboard box filled with her pots and pans. What were the thieves trying to find in her poor dwelling?

Shedding tears, she began to clean with skilled hands. Her entire childhood she had cleaned up after her alcoholic mother and her guests, when the mother couldn't move a limb. Her mother didn't need much—that new husband of hers killed her with a bottle a day, as Lelia found out years later from the neighbor. That neighbor was terrified of the fruit seller and his jolly family: her mother-in-law once yelled at him about the noise and filth, and in reply he slammed her head against the wall, and a week later the old thing passed away from a stroke. (They kept her death quiet, hoping to get a three-room apartment when their communal flat was broken up, but in the end they didn't.) The fruit seller sold Lelia's room and now resides in a cottage outside the city, or so they say.

For a long time Lelia crawled through the mess. At the same time she was glad that the children didn't see what had been done to their home, and prayed that Tamilla had taken them inside—the weather was extremely cold.

Nikita's hour was approaching—another reason Lelia couldn't bring the children home. Tamilla knew about his visits and occasionally let them sit out the two hours at her apartment.

At a quarter past seven, when Lelia was about to go upstairs to fetch the children, she heard the key turn in the keyhole. Lelia grabbed a butter knife from the kitchen, turned off the lights, and stood by the door. The door opened, and the light from the stairs fell on the heavily painted face of Nikita's sister. She saw the shadow by the door and froze. Automatically she half-closed the door behind her and turned on the light.

Lelia stared at her, seething with rage. Nikita's sister did the same.

"How come you're still alive?" the sister gasped. "Here I am, running around collecting inheritance papers, and you're still kicking. Nikita assured me you were all goners!"

"What inheritance?" Lelia muttered.

"Ours!" The sister yelled. "Get out of here while you still can. I'm going to call my boys." And she took out her cell phone.

Here Lelia produced the knife, issued a long, multilayered expletive, and promised the sister she'd cut her up like a hog if she didn't explain what was happening.

The woman, who was stocky and fat and could overpower Lelia with one hand had it not been for the knife, dropped the phone back into her purse and told her that yes, she and her mother were the heirs, and there was a will, with stamps and signatures.

"Whose heirs? Your grandmother's?"

"What grandmother, you idiot? Nikita's! Before he died he signed everything over to us. This apartment, that is."

"I see. . . . So it was you. You were looking for papers and turned my home upside down."

"What do you think—I'd be tiptoeing around your shit?" And the woman nodded to someone behind Lelia's back. When Lelia turned around, the woman pushed her back against the wall and stepped on the knife, which had dropped to the floor. Lelia kicked wherever she could reach. Upstairs Jerry heard the commotion and barked loudly. He knew something was happening but couldn't unlock the door.

"Help!" Lelia screamed, then stopped. God forbid Tamilla should bring down the children. The woman pressed the knife to Lelia's throat and commanded her to put her hands behind her back. Blood streamed down Lelia's neck. The woman tied her hands with the phone cord and pushed her toward the bathroom.

"Keep walking," she was saying, "I don't have all night. Mommy and I found a villa on Cyprus, a ten-minute walk from the beach, with orange trees in the yard! We have buyers for this shithole; they agreed to wait six months as the inheritance law requires. After that we will be the rightful heirs! We just need to get rid of your crap and then renovate the place. Can you walk any faster?" And she smacked Lelia on the head with the knife.

Lelia fell. Blood flowed in thick waves. The woman kept talking, trying to get Lelia up.

"Up you go, I said! Anyway, we are Nikita's heirs. Tomorrow, movers are coming to throw everything out. For my own apartment I'll strangle anyone—or hire a boy to do it. It doesn't cost much."

She kicked Lelia in the face.

"By the way, your house in Sergiev is ours, too. Last week Nikita came to see us with his new wife and told us about his new dacha. We asked about your funeral, but he said he wasn't going to collect you and the brats from the morgue. Do you know he had been married for a year? They both died suddenly. The corpses looked like some monsters from *Jurassic Park*."

The woman took a breath.

"So you broke into my house in Sergiev, just like that?" Lelia asked weakly.

"Not yours—ours! They were bringing out a casket with some Lida when we came."

"Lida? That's my aunt!"

"Her family was all over the place. They cleaned you out: bookcase, refrigerator, everything. We shooed them away."

"Poor Lida must have accepted a box of chocolates from my husband. . . ."

"Not your husband! Your marriage was fake; the children weren't his. We can prove it; we can do the test."

"How did he die?" Lelia whispered, dreading the answer.

"Ah, you want to know everything before you go! Listen up, then. The last thing he told me was that he regretted not killing me and Mom. So I wished him a bon voyage. I didn't believe him, thought he was drunk. Wife's already dead, he screamed. She and Nikita both gobbled down some chocolates, from his freezer, the wife admitted before she croaked. He said he didn't have an antidote. Like in Edgar Allan Poe, he said. 'The Cask of Amontillado.'"

Lelia gasped. Nikita's "wife" must have taken the chocolates from the freezer that night when she heard them leave.

"Well," continued the horrible hag, "he got his punishment for Grandma, didn't he?"

"You mean, he poisoned your grandmother, too?"

"That's nothing. Do you know how many have died recently at his department? Two. Why? They had an opening for a senior fellow, but Nikita didn't get it because of them."

"But why did it come up, that opening?"

"Their chief died, an old dude. But that was without my brother's help—the old man was at the sanatorium."

"Where Nikita visited him? I remember."

"You got it, finally? You should've stayed away from our family. Here, I'll drag you."

The hag bent over Lelia and tried to grab her ankles, but her fat belly was in the way. She was panting loudly.

"Listen to me, Sveta," whispered Lelia with her last bit of strength. "I know he gave you three pills of poison to be tested. He kept saying that he owed you three thousand dollars. So you gave him one of those pills?"

"Stupid cow," Sveta yelled back, unbending with difficulty. "My own brother! That's it. I'm not going to soil my hands with you. I'll just throw you in the tub and tell the boys to finish you off. . . ."

She was looking around for something to tie Lelia's feet with.

"Listen to me: my children are alive, and they are your only heirs. You'll never have a husband; your boyfriends want only your money, like that Valera of yours. . . ."

"It's you, stupid whore, who'll never marry! What children are you talking about?"

"My son and daughter are alive and being watched by friends."

"Yeah, right." Sveta grabbed Lelia by the ankles,

but Lelia kicked her in the shin and the killer jumped back.

Gasping, Lelia continued her prophesying.

"It's too late for you to have children, obviously; plus, consider your syphilis."

Sveta's tongue froze. Nobody was supposed to know about her illness, except her mother, who let it slip to Nikita.

"I'm getting my boys," she screamed, and reached for the phone, but her fingers were sticky with Lelia's blood, and she kept missing the buttons.

Lelia got up slowly and advanced toward the killer, screaming that she knew nurses at the venereal clinic that treated Sveta (unsuccessfully).

"I know nurses everywhere," Lelia screamed, "so take care when you're getting your shots!"

Sveta choked with indignation. "Ah," she finally breathed out. "You made me all filthy. Into the bathroom. *Now!*"

Poking Lelia with the knife, Sveta shoved her into the bathroom and locked the door. Then, with bloodied fingers, she began dialing the number.

At that moment they heard Tamilla's voice in the hall. "Lelia! The children are tired and want to go home! I need to take Jerry out!"

Of course. The killer forgot to lock the door.

"Help! Police! Don't come in! Help!" screamed

Lelia in the dark bathroom, her hands tied behind her back. "Don't bring the children! Help! Murder!"

She couldn't see what happened, but heard Sveta's bloodcurdling scream. In a single motion the huge beast leaped across the hall and knocked the killer to the ground.

Among Friends

'm a direct person, always smirking and poking fun when we all get together at Marisha and Serge's on Fridays. Everyone comes. If one of us misses a Friday, it must be because he or she couldn't get away, or has been banished by the enraged Marisha or the entire gang. Andrey the informer, for example, was banished for a long time after socking Serge in the eye. Can you imagine? Serge, our bright star, our precious genius! Serge has figured out the working principle of flying saucers. That's right. I looked at his calculations: some universal point of departure, some this, some that—a bunch of nonsense, if you ask me, and I'm very smart. You see, Serge doesn't read about his subject; he relies on intuition—a mistake, in my opinion. Some time ago he intuited a way to increase the energy efficiency of a steam engine from 15 to 70 percent—a miracle. He was feted, presented to the members of the Academy of Science. One academician finally came to his senses and pointed out that this very principle was discovered a hundred years ago and described in a college textbook on page such and such;

the same textbook explains why it doesn't work. The miracle was canceled; 70 percent became 36, also purely theoretical, but by this point a special unit had been set up at the Academy to study Serge's so-called discovery, and Serge was invited to be the head. A mass rejoicing among our friends followed—Serge didn't even have a PhD! But Serge chose to stay at his miserable job in the Oceanography Institute, because they had been planning an expedition with stops in Boston, Hong Kong, Vancouver, and Montreal—six months of sun and freedom—and Serge hoped to go, too.

The 36 percent unit, in the meantime, began operating at a leisurely pace. They fetched Serge once or twice for a consultation, but soon got the hang of the utopian project: to replace all modern technology with an impossibly efficient steam engine. This stupendous goal was to be accomplished by five people jammed into a single room, who divided work hours between the cafeteria and smoking room. In addition, the head of the unit, who was hired instead of Serge and who did have a PhD, was having a child on the side any moment, and the parents of the woman had filed a complaint against him. He spent his workdays screaming on the phone in the same room with the other staff. Our Lenka was the lab assistant there; she told us all the gossip. As far as Lenka could tell, no one once mentioned Serge's principle. All that had been accomplished was a draft of an application to use the lab for three hours after midnight, when the building is closed, as if anyone were going to be there.

Serge's bid for sun and freedom also came to nothing. In his Party questionnaire he wrote that he wasn't a member of the Komsomol, but in his original job application he had written that he was. The Party committee responsible for approving everyone who went abroad compared the paperwork and discovered that Serge had simply stopped paying his dues, just like that, and that couldn't be fixed by anything, so the committee didn't admit him. All this was told to us by Andrey, who also worked there, and who stopped by at Marisha's one Friday night, drank some vodka, and then revealed in a fit of honesty that he'd promised to inform on the other members of that expedition—that's how the Party committee had admitted him. He said we shouldn't tell him anything, even though he had promised to inform only on the ship and not on dry land. True enough, Andrey left with the expedition and brought back a small plastic dildo, purchased in Hong Kong. Why so small? He didn't have money for a bigger one. I said that Andrey had bought it for his daughter. Serge was there, too, looking distracted, for he had spent the last six months in Leningrad with a bunch of lowly assistants, taking care of the expedition's correspondence. All this, you must understand, happened some time ago, back in the days when Marisha and Serge stood together and lamented Serge's career. But those days of friendship and understanding are long gone; these days, God knows what mess is happening, and still every Friday we come, as though magnetized, to the little apartment on Stulin Street and drink all night.

In the beginning, "we" meant, first of all, our hosts, Serge and Marisha, and their daughter, Sonya, who stoically slept in the next room through the racket. (All three are now my relatives—such is the absurd result of our communal life.) Then there was myself, for no good reason; my husband, Kolya, Serge's oldest friend; Andrey the informer, first with his wife, then with a string of temporary women, and finally with a new wife, Nadya; then there was Zhora, whose mother is Jewish, something no one but me ever mentions; and then Tanya, a blond Valkyrie, Serge's favorite—sometimes, when especially drunk, he stroked her hair.

Once, there was also Lenka, a D-size beauty, twenty years old. At first Lenka behaved like a common con artist: at the record store, where she worked, she talked herself into Marisha's favor, borrowed twenty rubles from her, and disappeared. Later Lenka reappeared without four front teeth but with Marisha's twenty rubles and said she had been at the hospital, where they told her she could never have children. Marisha showered her with affection, Serge found her a position at the 36 percent unit, and Lenka replaced her missing teeth and married a young Jewish dissident who turned out to be the son of a famous underground cosmetologist, a fantastically rich woman. According to Lenka, the contents of a single closet in her new home could feed us all for the rest of our days. Lenka, however, didn't appreciate her new comfortable position and continued to run around the seediest holes. Finally she declared that her husband's family was immigrating to the United States, via Vienna, but she wasn't going with them. So she went and divorced her nice Jewish husband, and at our gatherings she developed a new habit of flopping on the lap of every boy in turn. Only Serge she considered untouchable, because he belonged to her deity, Marisha.

But Andrey the informer wasn't untouchable, and Lenka regularly mocked him by flopping on his lap, so his super-young new wife, Nadya, turned purple and fled to the kitchen. That Nadya was just eighteen, even younger than Lenka, and looked like a corrupt schoolgirl. No surprise there: as Andrey's previous wife told everyone, Andrey was impotent. Only something like this Nadya could arouse his interest. When this corrupt nymphet got married, however, she changed her tune and became a plain housewife: what she cooked, what she bought. Her only remaining perversity was a wandering eyeball:

at moments of stress it would literally fall out and hang over her cheek like a hard-boiled egg. Andrey, I suppose, lived for these dramatic moments: he would grab Nadya, carry her to the ER, and on those nights, I imagine, he was able to perform.

Andrey's life with his previous wife, Aniuta, was similarly punctuated by high drama, involving the attacks of her so-called venomous womb. This venomous womb, which prevented them from having children, was a popular subject among us, their friends. By then we all had had children: Zhora had three, I had my Alesha, and if I missed two Fridays in a row they joked that I was in bed with child, a reference to my figure. Tanya had a son who as a baby crawled all over her, from breast to breast, the mother and child's favorite amusement. But Andrey and Aniuta were sentenced to childlessness, and we all pitied them; for the whole point was to live normally, to worry about feedings, childcare, illnesses, but then one night a week, on Friday, to escape the routine and relax so completely that the neighbors across the street would call the cops. Then one day, almost without any physical change, Aniuta gave birth to a daughter. That night Andrey bought two bottles of vodka, he and Serge invited my Kolya, and the three of them spent the night boozing. That was the high point of his family life, and after that, I expect, Andrey forsook his conjugal duties for a long time, while Aniuta became an ordinary woman

without any venomous womb and expanded her circle
of friends, so to speak, especially when Andrey was
gone squealing for six months. Andrey found consolation in a string of gorgeous girlfriends, all of whom he
brought to Marisha's.

Lenka once flopped on my Kolya, too, and Marisha turned away abruptly and began to talk with
Zhora. This was when I first began to understand.
Lenka, I said, you've gone too far: Marisha's jealous of
you. Lenka just grinned and stayed on top of Kolya,
who drooped like a little flower. From that moment
on, Marisha's affection for Lenka began to cool, and
eventually Lenka disappeared from our gatherings.
Lenka never flopped on Zhora, because Zhora, like
many runty men, demonstrated constant sexual ex-
citement and was in love with all our girls—Marisha,
Tanya, and even frigid Lenka. Flirting with Zhora was
dangerous, as one incident demonstrated, when at the
end of a dance with Andrey's girlfriend, Zhora simply
grabbed her by the armpits and dragged her into the
next room, where he threw her on Sonya's little bed
(Sonya was at her grandmother's that night). Except
for the attacked woman, we all knew, of course, that
Zhora only played at being a ladies' man; that in reality he spent his nights writing a dissertation for his
wife and attending to his three children, and only on
Fridays did he throw on Casanova's cloak. But the

careful Lenka refused to play sexual games with Zhora, for then it would be two performances: she'd flop on his lap, and he'd have to grope her, which Lenka didn't enjoy—and neither did Zhora. But Lenka has long been gone, and when I mention her name it's received as another of my blunders.

Recently my memory grew hazy and I began losing my eyesight. How many years passed in our Friday gatherings? Ten? Fifteen? We heard of the political unrest in Czechoslovakia, then in China, then in Romania, then in Yugoslavia; after that came the news about the trials of the culprits, followed by the trials of those who had protested against the original trials, then the trials of those who had collected money to support the families of the incarcerated dissidents, but all these events rolled past our nest on Stulin Street.

Occasionally we had a visitor. One night the neighbors summoned the local patrolman to quiet the noise. On Fridays Marisha's door was always open, so this patrolman, Valera, barged in and demanded to see everyone's papers. None of our boys had a passport, and the girls Valera didn't ask, which led us to believe he was looking for someone. After days of nervous phone exchanges we decided that Valera was looking for a certain Lev, a naturalized American whose Russian visa had expired and so he could go to jail for a year. This Lev had been coasting from house to house, but I never saw him at Marisha's. Her neighbors—a couple of eternal students and their ever-changing lovers—accommodated him for a night, and he, by mistake, took the virginity of the government minister's daughter, a sophomore in the journalism department. Apparently the girl woke up covered in blood, panicked, and dragged her bloody mattress to the kitchen sink—they didn't even have a shower in that apartment. The neighbors told us all this with a laugh when they came the next day to borrow a ruble for vodka. The daughter, they said, was now looking high and low for Lev, considering him her intended after the Russian custom, but Lev disappeared from Stulin Street, and the patrolman wasted his visit.

The following Friday, however, Valera returned to turn off our boom box at five minutes past eleven and didn't leave. He stayed all night, watching in silence, as we drank. What he wanted remains unclear. Marisha was the first to find the right tone, and addressed him as a misunderstood, lonely young boy. (In that house, everyone was welcome and comforted, but few chose to impose.) Marisha offered Valera bread and cheese with dry wine—all they had on their poor table—and, followed by Serge, engaged him in a conversation. Valera answered their questions calmly and unselfconsciously. Serge asked, for example, if Valera had joined the police to get a Moscow registration, and he said no, he'd had registration before; he chose that neighborhood because of its toughness and because he knew karate. He'd had to quit the sport after an injury: during a practice he didn't signal to his opponent to stop. "What kind of signal?" I asked. "Well"—he blushed—"one has to cough or, pardon me, pass wind." I wanted to know how one can fart on demand, but Valera ignored me and proceeded to tell us that things were soon going to change back to where they were under Stalin, when we at least had some order.

We tried to subject Valera to the same mocking interrogation we inflicted on all our guests, but either he was very clever or we were too passive. He deftly avoided our hesitant questioning and revealed nothing of himself or of his work duties and instead went on and on about Stalin, and we were too afraid of his provocations to reveal our own political opinions. Who reveals them anyway? It was considered childish and rude, and so Valera remained untapped and unstudied, and at midnight we all slunk away, but Valera stayed on. Maybe he had nowhere else to spend his shift, or maybe he was in fact waiting for Lev—who knows? We all felt put on the rack. Lenka didn't sit on anyone's lap, and Zhora didn't shout "hey, virgins" at the passing schoolgirls; only I wouldn't shut up about the one subject he avoided, and he couldn't do anything—he introduced the subject himself, plus *fart* wasn't on the list of obscene words punishable with fifteen days of prison. I alone kept interrupting the flow of Serge's condescending questions, but Valera didn't give a damn about Serge's condescension and persisted in his dangerous speeches about the army and those who control it. "But still, tell us, do they teach you how to fart in the army?" I asked him again and again. "You, obviously, didn't learn the trick and sustained an injury. . . ." The army, Valera intoned in response, you can't begin to imagine; hands of gold they have, they know every weapon inside out. . . . Serge asked Valera how often he was on duty and where they gave him a room, and Marisha asked if he was married and had children. Tanya quietly commented on Valera's most idiosyncratic remarks, always addressing Zhora, who was half Jewish but looked entirely Jewish, as though supporting him in this difficult situation. Zhora was the only one with a passport, and Valera read his data out loud: Georgy Alexandrovich Perevoshchikov, ethnically Russian.

I was curious to see how Andrey the informer would react to Valera's presence, but he was calm and reserved. When Valera turned off the music, Andrey had to sit down next to his Nadya, who despite looking like a perverse teenager was dying of banal jealousy. Her father, however, was an army colonel on the rise, and she listened to Valera's macho speeches through the prism of his lowly rank of lieutenant. She relaxed, went out to call a girlfriend, and then walked off with her Andrey, and Valera said nothing. Who knows, maybe we all could leave and he would have allowed that. But then again, maybe he wouldn't. In the end Marisha gave up and went to sleep on the floor in Sonya's room, and Serge stayed to ply Valera with diuretic herbal tea. Yet in the course of the night, Serge reported later, Valera hadn't once left the room to pee. Serge held it, too, afraid that Valera would search the room in his absence.

That night Kolya and I made it in time for the subway and, on coming home at half past one, discovered that Alesha was snoozing in front of the television, which was transmitting only static. When I put him to bed, he said he was afraid of the dark and of sleeping alone in the house. The lights were on in every room. He didn't used to be afraid, but then my father, his grandfather, was still with us. My father died recently, three months after my mother. She died from an illness that began with blindness, the same illness I now seem to have. My parents had raised him, surrounded him with love and care. And now he is to remain completely alone, for I am going to leave soon, too, and as for Kolya, I can't rely on him to take care of our son. Kolya, so generous and kind to the others, quickly gets bored and irritable at home and yells at Alesha, especially at mealtimes. In addition, Kolya was preparing to leave us, and not just for anyone—for Marisha.

Many years, I'll repeat, passed over our peaceful Friday gatherings. Andrey the informer turned from a golden-haired Paris into a father, then an abandoned husband, then the owner of a condominium bought for his new wife by her father the colonel, and finally an alcoholic. But as in college, he remained in love with Marisha, who knew and appreciated it. All other women in his life were just replacements. Once or twice a year Andrey performed a sacred ritual, a slow dance with Marisha.

Zhora grew from an unruly undergraduate into a penniless research fellow with three children, a future star of his field, but his essence remained unchanged, and that essence was his ardent love for Marisha, who had always loved Serge and no one else.

My Kolya also worshipped Marisha. All our boys lost their heads over Marisha in our freshman year, and their competition continued up until the shocking moment when Serge, who was married to Marisha and alone had rights to her, suddenly up and left her for another woman, whom he had adored, it turned out, since grade school. It happened on New Year's Eve, in the middle of the charades: he simply got up with an announcement that he must call his beloved, to wish her a happy New Year. Just like that.

We were all deeply shaken, for if the boys worshipped Marisha, we all of us collectively worshipped Marisha and Serge as a couple. Many years ago Serge fell in love with Marisha and offered her marriage, but Marisha was seduced by a charming scoundrel, a certain Jean, and rejected Serge's pure first love. After Jean had left her, she crawled back to Serge and proposed marriage to him, forever rejecting the idea of erotic love on the side. She used to say that Serge was a sacred crystal vessel. ("Not easy to make love to," I would remark.)

In those early days we lived for camping trips, drinking by the bonfire, mocking everything and everyone. The only aspects of the sexual sphere that caught our attention were my white swimming suit, which turned transparent in the water, and the absence of a lavatory at our camping site, because Zhora complained that in the ocean poop didn't swim away. Romantic Andrey walked three miles to the TB sanatorium to dance with the patients; Serge expressed his masculinity through scuba diving. At night I could hear rhythmic knocking coming from their tent, but her entire married life, Marisha remained a jittery creature with shining eyes, which didn't speak well of Serge's abilities.

The sexual flame that flickered around Marisha

in combination with her inaccessibility held our circle together for so long. The girls loved Serge and wanted to replace Marisha, but at the same time pitied Marisha and wouldn't betray her. Everything and everyone was full of their undivided, irresistible love, but Serge, the only one with the right of access to the beautiful Marisha, was restless with anger, and one time this ulcer partially broke. We were sitting at the table discussing sexual themes—innocently, for we were pure people and could discuss anything innocently. Someone mentioned the book *Sexopathology* by a Polish author. Now, that book was an entirely new phenomenon for our society, where every citizen lived as if on a desert island. In the book, I announced, sex is divided into three parts: in the first, the spouses arouse one another by stroking their earlobes! Did you know that, Serge? Everyone froze, and Serge began to shake and sputter and scream that his attitude toward me had always been deeply negative—but what did I care? I knew I had hit the mark.

All this had taken place before Serge rediscovered the love of his life and before the patrolman Valera began his vigils on Stulin Street, and also before I found out that I was losing my eyesight, and definitely before I realized that Marisha was jealous of my Kolya. Suddenly all the knots became untied. Serge stopped sleeping on Stulin Street; our Friday gatherings moved to the room Tanya shared with her teenage son, who was pathologically jealous of her and who had to be moved to Stulin Street, where he spent the night with Sonya. I remarked that it would do them both good, they should get used to sleeping with each other, but as usual no one paid me any attention.

In between Fridays we were overtaken by a wave of tragic events. Marisha's father was run over by a car outside her house—he was heavily intoxicated, as the autopsy showed. That night he had had a conversation with Serge, man to man, about his decision to leave Marisha. The conversation took place early, when Sonya was still awake. They were keeping from Sonya that Serge had left the family. Serge came home after work and stayed until nine to put Sonya to bed, then went back to his childhood erotic ideal. Poor Marisha's father, who himself was onto his second family, walked in on them right in the middle of this fake family time, said some useless things, and uselessly perished under the car at nine thirty, when there is no traffic.

During that time my mother melted from 160 pounds to 70. She held up bravely, but right at the end her doctors decided to look for a nonexistent ulcer: they opened her up, then by mistake sewed a bowel to the stomach muscle, leaving her to die with an open wound the size of a fist. When they rolled her out to me, dead, crudely stitched up with a gaping hole in her belly, something happened: I couldn't understand how this could have been done to a human being, let alone my mother, and began to imagine that my mama was somewhere else, that this couldn't be her.

Kolya wasn't with me that day. He and I had separated five years earlier but didn't pay for the divorce and continued to live like roommates, as is often done. After my mother's funeral, though, he informed me that he had paid his share and suggested that I pay, too, and so I did. Three months later my father died from a heart attack, in his sleep: I got up to put a blanket over Alesha and saw that Papa wasn't breathing. I went back to bed, waited till morning, and saw them both off: Alesha to school and Papa to the morgue.

So I missed several Fridays, and then came Easter, when by tradition we congregate at my house. My parents used to help me with the cooking; then they and Alesha would travel for ninety minutes to our allotment, where they would stay the night in an unheated shack so my guests could party all night in our house. This year I told Alesha that he was going to the allotment alone: he was big enough—seven years old—and knew his way there perfectly. I also forbade him to come back and ring the bell under any circumstances.

That morning I took Alesha for the first time to visit my parents' grave. He helped me carry water; we planted some daisies. Alesha overcame his initial fear and took pleasure in planting flowers in our clean, dry soil—I had my parents cremated, so there are just urns with ashes, nothing to be afraid of—and then we washed our hands and ate our bread, apples, and Easter eggs, leaving the crumbs for the birds. Everywhere around us people were drinking and eating at their family plots—we have preserved the tradition of visits to the cemetery on Easter, when the air smells of early spring and the dead are lying in their neat graves, remembered and toasted; and we will all go down the same road, everything ending for us with paper flowers, ceramic portraits, birds in the air, and bright Easter eggs on the ground. On the way home, on the subway and bus, everyone was tipsy but in an amicable, peaceful way, as though we had just peeked beyond the grave, seen fresh air and plastic flowers, and drunk to them.

From the cemetery Alesha set out without rest for the allotment, and I went back home to start dough for cabbage pies—all I could afford that year. A cabbage pie, a pie with Mama's jam, potato salad, boiled eggs, grated beets, a little cheese and salami—good enough. My salary is small, and I couldn't expect Kolya to chip in—he had practically moved in with his parents and on his rare visits yelled at Alesha that he didn't eat right, didn't sit right, dropped crumbs on the floor, watched television all the time, didn't read anything, and was growing up to be God knows what. This pointless rant was in fact a scream of envy inspired by Sonya, Marisha and Serge's daughter, who sang, composed music, went to the elite music school where the competition was three hundred students per slot, read since age two, and wrote poetry and prose. At the end of the day Kolya did love Alesha, but he would have loved him a lot more if Alesha were talented and handsome, good at his studies, and popular with his peers. Right now Kolya saw a version of himself, which drove him up the wall. Like Kolya, our son had poor teeth, which hadn't come in completely. Also, he had never adjusted to his orphaned status after losing my parents, and ate sloppily, without chewing, dropping large pieces on his lap and spilling everything. In addition he began to wet his bed. Kolya flew like a corkscrew out of our family nest in order not to see his little son drenched in pee, shaking in wet underpants. When Kolya saw this for the first time, he slapped Alesha with the back of his hand, and Alesha fell back into his filthy bed, relieved to be punished. I just smirked and left for work. That day I had an appointment with an ophthalmologist, who diagnosed the same hereditary illness that killed my mother. (She didn't name it, but she did prescribe the same drops and the same tests.) So how could I care that Alesha was peeing himself and that Kolya had slapped him? New horizons opened up before me, and I began to take measures toward saving my son from the fate of an orphan.

That Easter day, after coming back from the cemetery, I baked my pies, extended the dinner table, covered it with a tablecloth, arranged plates and wineglasses, salads, cold cuts, and bread. In the evening, with Alesha gone, I received my slightly embarrassed guests. They all came because of Marisha, who was too brave and too proud not to show her face. Serge was there, too, and my newly divorced husband, Kolya, with his ruined teeth. He went straight into the kitchen to unpack everyone's contributions to the table: boiled potatoes, pickled cucumbers, and many bottles of wine—clearly, they planned to party all night. And why not? There was an empty apartment at their disposal, plus the titillating fact that Marisha and my Kolya had been married the day before. Serge behaved as usual, only a little ravenous for booze; he and Zhora immediately retreated to celebrate. Lenka had long been gone; someone saw her on the subway wrapped tightly in a shawl: she said she had delivered a stillborn baby but didn't complain, only mentioned her breast milk arrived. Andrey the informer put on a record; his underage wife, Nadya, began to play mother of the family, telling me in detail how much child support

Andrey was paying, and that he didn't want to defend his thesis because his entire raise would go to his former wife and daughter and so on. Tanya the Valkyrie walked in, flashing her eyes and white teeth at me; I asked if her son was sharing Sonya's bed, but she just brayed.

"For you, Tanya, it's nothing, but Marisha has a daughter—have you taught her how not to get pregnant?"

"What's going on?" Nadya jumped in.

"Nadya," I asked her, "is it true you have a glass eye?"

"She's always been like that," explained shining Tanya, and Andrey added that his attitude toward me had always been deeply negative, but I ignored the informing scum.

Serge and Zhora, already drunk, emerged from the kitchen, and Kolya stepped out of our former bedroom—God knows what he was doing there.

"Kolya, have you finished selecting sheets for your new marital bed?" I addressed him. I knew by his reaction that I was right.

"Marisha," I continued, "do you have enough sheets to sleep with my husband? Mine are all ruined. Kolya decided to wash the sheets for the first time in his life, and he boiled them: all the sperm cooked, and now it looks like clouds in the sky."

They all laughed and sat down to eat. Then it was Serge's turn. Mumbling drunkenly, he argued with

Zhora about the theory of a certain Riabkin: Serge attacked it viciously, and Zhora defended it, but without enthusiasm. Finally Zhora grew tired and agreed with Serge with obvious condescension, and suddenly we saw that our genius Serge was just a failing, unrecognized scholar, while bedraggled Zhora was a true rising star, for nothing betrays success like condescension toward one's peers.

"Zhora, when are you defending your doctoral thesis?" I asked him at random, and guessed correctly, for Zhora took the bait and told us excitedly that his pre-defense was on Tuesday and the actual defense whenever they could find a slot in the schedule.

For a moment everyone was silent, and then began to drink. They drank to the point of blacking out. Andrey began to complain that his local Party committee wouldn't allow them to buy a three-room apartment, to the displeasure of Nadya's papa, who was recently promoted to general and wanted to shower her with presents—if she agreed to study and hold off on a child. Nadya pouted that she wanted a baby, but no one listened to her. Marisha and Kolya were talking quietly, probably deciding when Kolya should pick up the rest of his things and where they were going to keep them while Marisha's apartment was being exchanged for a room for Serge and a small one-bedroom for Marisha, so that Sonya could have a private room for her music, and Serge could have somewhere to live with his child-hood love, and Marisha could sleep with my husband.

"Marisha," I asked her, "how do you like my house? Do you want to move in here? Alesha and I will live where you tell us—we don't need much. You may keep all my things, too."

"Idiot!" Andrey yelled. "All Marisha thinks about is how not to take anything from you!"

"But why not? Go ahead, take it. Alesha's going to an orphanage. I've made arrangements—I found one in Borovsk, a long way from here."

"Let's get out of here. I'm sick of this show," protested the informer, but as Andrey got up to leave, the others didn't stir—they wanted to stay for the curtain.

I reached for the papers on the bookshelf and showed them to Kolya. He took one look and tore everything up.

"Idiot, shameless idiot," spat Andrey.

I leaned back in my chair. "Help yourselves, dear guests," I told them. "I'll be right back with the pies."

"Fine," said Serge, and back to drinking they went. Andrey put on another record, and Serge invited his former wife, Marisha, for a dance. Marisha blushed and threw me a guilty glance. So I had already become their collective conscience, I thought.

The party went into high gear, with everyone drinking, singing, dancing, and shouting; only Kolya was unoccupied. He came up to me and asked, "Where's Alesha?"

"Out," I said.

"But it's past midnight!"

He went out into the hall, then detoured into the bathroom and stayed there for a long time. In the meantime, Marisha, who had drunk too much, couldn't think of anything better to do than to lean out of the kitchen window and throw up the beet salad on the wall of my building.

Ruined pies, cigarette butts, unfinished salads, apple cores, empty bottles under the couch, Nadya weeping and holding her eye, and Andrey dancing with Marisha in his arms, his annual sacred ritual, which Nadya witnessed for the first time—and it shocked her to the point of losing an eye.

Then Andrey quickly got dressed and dressed Nadya—the subway was about to stop running for the night. Serge and Zhora were also getting dressed. Kolya finally emerged from the bathroom and lay down on the couch, but was roused by Zhora and led to the door. And at the end of the procession walked beaming Tanya. I opened the door for them, and they all saw Alesha, who was sleeping outside on the steps.

Thus began the final act. I jumped outside and punched the sleeping child on the face so hard he started spouting blood from his nose and choking on blood and snot. Screaming, "How dare you come back when I told you not to," I continued to pummel my son, but they grabbed me and shoved me back into the apartment, holding the door while I kicked and yelled. I could hear them shouting; someone was weeping; Nadya was promising to strangle me with her bare hands. I could hear Kolya, on the way down, calling Alesha's name, swearing to take him away from me—anywhere, it didn't matter where. My calculations were correct: these people, who will rip out each other's throats without blinking, couldn't stand the sight of a child's blood.

I locked the door, turned off the light, tiptoed to the kitchen window, and looked out over Marisha's vomit. Soon the whole gang marched out; Kolya was carrying Alesha! They were talking excitedly, high on their righteousness, waiting for the last one, Andrey, who was holding the door. Nadya wept and screamed hysterically that I must be stripped of my maternal rights. Their drunken voices echoed throughout the neighborhood. They even flagged down a cab! Kolya, Alesha, and Marisha sat in the back, Zhora in the front. He'll be the one paying, I thought, as always, but why should I care? They'll all get home, somehow.

Of course they won't sue me; that's not their style. They'll hide Alesha from me, surround the abused child with love and attention. The most enduring affection, I foresee, will come from Andrey and his childless wife, Nadya. Tanya will take Alesha to the seacoast in the summer; Kolya, who tonight took Alesha in his arms, is not the same Kolya who slapped his little son for wetting his bed—he'll be a decent father from now on. Marisha, too, will love and pity my talentless, toothless boy. Zhora, who'll become a famous professor, will throw him a few crumbs and maybe help him get into college. Now, Serge is another matter. He will end up living with the only person he truly loves, his own daughter, his crazy love for whom will continue to lead him through life by dark corners and underground passages until he understands what's happening and gives up other women for the one he himself brought into the world. Such things do happen, and when it happens to Serge, my friends will find themselves in a serious predicament. But that won't happen for another eight years, and in the meantime Alesha will grow stronger and smarter. I've arranged his fate at a very cheap price: I simply sent him to the allotment without the key to the shack and forbade him to ring the bell or knock—he understands what *don't* means. My performance, the beating of an innocent child, threw Alesha into the protective arms of his indignant new parents, who otherwise would have sent him to an orphanage upon my death and barely tolerated his visits in their new home.

That's how I planned it, and that's how it will happen. And I'm glad that this odd family will live in Alesha's home, not he in theirs; it's better for him this way. Very soon I'll be gone; Alesha, I hope, will visit me on the first day of Easter at the cemetery, like I showed him earlier today. I think he'll come—he's a very smart boy. There, among the kindly drunken crowd, with their painted eggs and plastic wreaths, he'll think about his mother, and forgive her. My son, my Alesha, will forgive me, for not letting him say good-bye at the end, for leaving him without a mother's blessing, covered in blood, at the mercy of my so-called friends. That way it was best—for everyone. I'm smart, and I know.

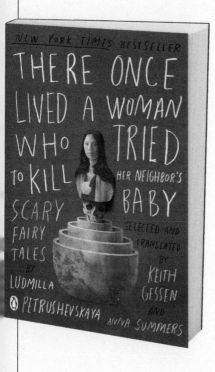